Deniz Kavukçuoğlu

ZARİFE

Translated by **Alvin Parmar**

Milet Publishing
Smallfields Cottage, Cox Green
Rudgwick, Horsham, West Sussex
RH12 3DE England
info@milet.com
www.milet.com
www.milet.co.uk

First English edition published by Milet Publishing in 2013
Copyright © Milet Publishing, 2013
ISBN 978 1 84059 855 1

First published in Turkish as *Zarife* in 2003

Funded by the Turkish Ministry of Culture and Tourism TEDA Project

Printed and bound in Turkey by Ertem Matbaası

Deniz Kavukçuoğlu

Deniz Kavukçuoğlu was born in Istanbul in 1943. At the age of 20, he went to Germany to complete his studies. While there, he studied philosophy under Ernst Bloch at the University of Tübingen for two years, sociology and the history of European workers' movements at Heidelberg University for two years, and economics at the University of Erlangen-Nuremberg. He remained in Germany because he was stripped of his Turkish citizenship after the 1971 military coup, and worked in management positions in various companies until he returned to Turkey in 1992. He has been the general coordinator of the Istanbul Book Fair since 1993 and has had a column in *Cumhuriyet* newspaper since 1996. Kavukçuoğlu has had thirteen books published. His short story collection *Something Funny to Write About* was published in English by Milet. He lives in Moda, Istanbul.

Alvin Parmar

Alvin Parmar was born in England in 1976. After studying French and Arabic at Cambridge, he spent ten years in Istanbul, where he learned Turkish and got involved in literary translation. He has over ten published translations to his name, including *The Disenchanted* by Mehmet Eroğlu, *Something Funny to Write About* by Deniz Kavukçuoğlu, *Kind-hearted Sinners* by Cezmi Ersöz, *A Midlife Dream* by Erendiz Atasü, and eleven stories in *Europe in Women's Short Stories from Turkey*, all published by Milet. Two plays that he translated have been performed in New York.

Editorial Notes

Throughout the stories in this novel, we have retained the Turkish for several types of terms, including personal names, honorifics, place names and foods, among others. We have used the English spelling of Istanbul, rather than its Turkish spelling, İstanbul, because the English version is so commonly known. For the Turkish terms, we have used italics in their first instance and then normal text for subsequent instances. We have not italicized the Turkish honorifics that form part of a name, such as Bey and Hanım, to avoid splitting the name visually with a style change. Lists of the Turkish honorifics and foods that appear in the book follow, along with a guide to Turkish pronunciation.

Turkish Honorifics

Abla: Older sister, also used as an honorific for women.

Amca: Uncle, also used to express respect.

Bey: A respectful term of address used after a man's first name.

Efendi: A title of courtesy, equivalent to the English 'sir', literally meaning lord or master.

Hanım: A respectful term of address used after a woman's first name.

Hanımefendi: A respectful way of addressing a woman without using her first name.

Hanımkızım: A polite and slightly old-fashioned term used to address a young lady.

Teyze: Aunt, also used to express respect.

Teyzeciğim: Auntie, also used to express respect and affection.

Turkish Foods

Börek: Filled savory pastry.

Döner: Kebab cut from meat on a gyrating grill.

Gözleme: Filled pancake cooked on a griddle.

Haydari: Yogurt with garlic and fresh herbs.

Kol böreği: Rolled savory pastry.

Meyhane: A traditional Turkish tavern.

Meze: Turkish dishes of small starters or hors d'œuvres.

Poğaça: Savory pastry buns filled with meat or cheese.

Rakı: Turkish aniseed spirit drink.

Su böreği: Savory pastry, often filled with cheese and parsley, cooked in water before being oven-baked.

Tarator: A dip sauce generally eaten with fried fish and squid made of walnuts, lemon juice or vinegar, garlic, herbs and yogurt.

Guide to Turkish Pronunciation

Turkish letters that appear in the book and which may be unfamiliar are shown below, with a guide to their pronunciation.

c   as *j* in 'just'

ç   as *ch* in 'child'

ğ   silent, but lengthens the preceding vowel

ı   as *a* in 'along'

ö   as German ö in 'Köln', or French *œ* in 'œuf'

ş   as *sh* in 'ship'

ü   as German ü in 'fünf', or French *u* in 'tu'

Zarife

I met her on Barbaros Boulevard at the Bosporus Bridge exit towards evening one rainy April day in 1993. She was standing on the foot-path, waving at the cars going past slowly because of the traffic at the entrance to the bridge. Every time I went past there, I always saw students hitchhiking and at first, I thought she was one of them. I stopped my car a bit further along and she ran up, poked her head in the open window, and asked if I would give her a lift. I told her to hop in and she did.

She had an innocent face. Her neck reminded me of the swanlike neck of Audrey Hepburn, who had adorned the dreams of my faraway youth, and I had seen every one of her films. My passenger's long black hair spilled over onto her shoulders; it had collected raindrops at its ends. I started the car and asked her with a smile where I could drop her off.

"Wherever you want. You can even take me out to dinner if you like!"

I was taken aback. We started chatting. Her name was Zarife and she was the daughter of a bricklayer who had moved from Sivas to Istanbul at the end of the fifties. She was living with her mother, her father and her two brothers, one older and one younger, in one of

1

the slum areas overlooking Beykoz, and she had been working as a sales assistant in a leather shop in Mecidiyeköy for a while. She had left high school two years ago, but although she got good marks in the university entrance exams, she had not been able to continue her education for financial reasons. She did not seem to regret this though. "Life goes on," she said.

"Life goes on." Listening to her, I could understand that these words, which so often pop up in everyday conversation and which we have grown used to and no longer think about, had a different meaning for her. She was prepared to offer her body in exchange for being able to live a life that was beyond her means, I thought to myself. "Life goes on . . . I don't give a damn . . . I don't care . . ." She was very comfortable saying these things. She thought that it would be easy for other people to understand.

"What's the big deal?" she asked.

Her approach to life was nothing other than what someone looking at it from a different perspective would call whoring. But she had not been branded a whore yet and for some reason, she made you feel as if it was something else. Maybe it was just the winds blowing through the heart of this young girl with an innocent face, the winds that she wanted to fly away on, getting to me. She had so many justifications for choosing this path to take her to the life she longed for that she thought it proved her right!

Like everyone else, she too wanted to go to the up-market places in Istanbul: she wanted to go shopping in Nişantaşı or on Bağdat Street, to have fun in Etiler, Kuruçeşme and Çubuklu, to dance in the smart clubs that she had heard of and always wanted to go to but had never been able to, to dine at good restaurants and have a drink in the bars the magazines she had read made her curious about. You only have one time on this earth; you only have one life. So did she too not have the right to wake up to the morning sun on a boat in the middle of the azure in the Aegean or the Mediterranean?

She had found the solution in having relationships of varying length and taking her clothes off for men who desired her and who would tell her what she wanted to hear and let her live the life she wanted to live, albeit in dribs and drabs. She did not think about the consequences: she never dwelt on them, she just forgot. The more estranged she became from her body, the easier it was for her to surrender herself. Even if she did realize that the life she wanted and the life she already had and would be able to have were completely artificial, what else could she do, apart from forcing herself to think that those artificialities were real? And she was not taking money from anyone. Nor did she expect to. If there was anyone who paid anything in these relationships, it was she. She was paying for her dreams.

She had something about her that made you think, that forced you to question the people around you and the life you were leading. She was very surprised when I told her I would drop her off somewhere convenient. I stopped my car at the turn-off for Kızıltoprak. She got out without saying a word.

* * *

Seven years later, I was flicking between TV channels one night and I saw her on the screen in a celebrity gossip program. She had climbed up onto a table and was dancing in one of the smart clubs in Etiler. It was somewhere she had mentioned during our short car ride. She had said that she was curious about it and wanted to go there and enjoy herself. A very famous place where they say that you can buy marijuana, pills and cocaine in the toilets . . . She was out of it. It was as if in seven years that innocent face had aged seventeen years, but her features were still the same. I guess she did not hitchhike at bridges, live on the outskirts of Beykoz, or work behind the counter in a leather shop any more.

When the image on the screen changed, I thought to myself, if she had made some different life choices, who knows where she would be now? I would actually have liked to ask her this directly, but it will not be possible because in life our paths will never cross.

—Bülent Serdar

Zarife called Bülent Serdar a week after reading this article. She had read it in a hotel in Mersin. After coming back from a meal late one evening, she had asked the young man on reception for something to read. He looked everywhere, but could not find anything like what she had asked for, so he offered her his own newspaper. Flicking through it in bed back in her room, she saw her own name in the title of the top right-hand column of the page with the cartoons on; she was intrigued and read the article.

When she got back to Istanbul, she called the newspaper and spoke to Bülent Serdar. She said she wanted to meet him. He suggested a patisserie he went to several evenings a week: "If it's convenient for you, we can meet tomorrow in Taksim, in the café beneath the Marmara Hotel, at 4 o'clock."

Bülent Serdar went to the patisserie an hour early. He sat at one of the tables for two that looked out onto the square and asked the waiter for a filter coffee and a cognac. At first, Zarife's call had excited him, as a journalist. But the more hypotheses he dreamt up for why she had called him, the more his excitement turned into a dogged feeling of apprehension. She must be angry about his article. Thinking about it, he could see her point. He was wrong to have judged so harshly someone he had briefly met during a twenty-minute car journey seven years ago.

Soon she would be here, sitting across from him and having it out with him. None of the answers he had rehearsed in his head to the questions she might ask seemed convincing, not even to himself. She was going to ask him what gave him the right to call her a whore. What was he going to say? How could he answer that?

Maybe the real mistake was turning down her suggestion to go out for a meal seven years ago. He could have said yes and driven down the motorway via the Altunizade junction. An intimate dinner with a beautiful young girl like her overlooking Beylerbeyi would not have been such a bad thing. He would have taken her to a restaurant that was suitable for those purposes. She would have drunk *rakı*, just like all the young girls who want to grow up fast. First, the drinks would have arrived and then the modest *meze* tray. White cheese, melon, eggplant salad, spicy dip, *haydari* . . .

"How would you like your salad, sir?" the waiter would have asked. "A shepherd's salad, a seasonal salad or a lettuce salad?"

Then they would have started chatting: "It's a beautiful view, isn't it? It's good we came here." What else could they have talked about?

She would have told him about her longings and her dreams. How many times had he listened to tales of longings and dreams about lives that someone always wanted to live but that they never could? For some reason, girls like her always wanted to have other lives that were always the same as each other. As a sensitive, understanding and mature man, he would have made her think that he was listening carefully to what she was telling him, as if it was the first time he had heard such a story, and every time they made eye contact, he would have smiled at her.

Meanwhile, they would have finished their meze and it would be time for the main course. She would have asked for her meat to be well done, of course, just like all the other girls. When she heard him asking the waiter for his to be rare, she would have immediately asked how he could eat meat when it was bloody.

As always happens, his steak would have arrived well done, so he would have sent his plate back complaining that the meat was like leather. The girl would have stared into his eyes and said to him softly, "You must be a difficult man to please!"

Then, well aware that all the waiters and busboys were scrutinizing them from somewhere over by the door, he would have felt obliged to take her hand and stroke it. Hand in hand, they would have stared into each other's eyes for a while without saying a word. Then their coffee would have come. They would have got up and left the restaurant arm in arm, nodding to the headwaiter, the waiters and the busboys on their way out. As they were walking towards the car park, she would have snuggled up closely to him. When they were in the car with the doors closed, but before turning the headlights on, he would have kissed her. Because that was how it always happened . . . After he had turned the car headlights on and started the engine, he would have asked that classic question whose answer was a foregone conclusion: "Do you fancy coming up for a coffee?"

She would have wanted to take her shoes off when she came into the house and he would have told her there was no need and that he had cats anyway. But she would have taken them off all the same. After sitting down on the sofa and crossing her legs, she would have told him what sweet cats he had.

"Would you like a drink?"

There would have been no mention of coffee; they would have continued drinking what they had started off with in the restaurant.

"I won't mix drinks; I'll have a rakı."

After the second mouthful, the girl would have got up and started to wander around the room.

"You've got a nice house."

Then he would have listened to her interpretations of the oil paintings on the wall: "He's captured the light really well."

He had heard feeble interpretations like that so many times before. He would try to hide how fed up he was: "It's the artist's inner world, my dear. The artist's inner world," he would have replied, ". . . and that artist isn't a he, my dear, it's a she."

Then she would have looked at his books and CDs.

"You've got so many."

The thing was, they were all good books and good CDs, but for some reason, these young girls who longed for other lives always got fixated on the "many"; they did not seem to be able to strike the balance between "many" and "good". And that was why the conversation would have ended there.

"Why don't we go through to the other room?"

They would have gone into the bedroom, they would have had sex and then they would each have lit one cigarette. The mornings after nights like that, especially if it was not the weekend, were nightmares for him. To make matters worse, this girl worked at the other end of Istanbul in Mecidiyeköy. She would have to leave the house at the crack of dawn to be in time for work. So he would have had to get up before her, put the kettle on and make breakfast. And daylight stripped everyone so bare. Waking up as the day was dawning, having a shave, getting dressed . . . Then standing over her and saying, "Come on, it's time to get up, darling."

After she had left, he would not think anything more about this one-night woman.

But he had not done any of this with her. Was that not why he was here, in this patisserie? And had he not written that article precisely because he had not done any of this?

Could that beautiful woman he saw when he looked up as the waiter brought him his second cognac, the one who was hovering over by the rectangular glass counter in the middle of the patisserie looking around, be Zarife? She did not look like that girl with the innocent face he had met seven years ago or like that young woman from the fleeting image on the TV whose bleary eyes and disheveled long, black hair he had photographed in his memory.

She was wearing a tight long black skirt, slit at the back. A single-strand pearl necklace graced the décolleté of her long-sleeved blouse, which was also black. She was wearing her hair in a bun and had rose-red lipstick on. Her poise, her movements and her appearance were like an Andalucian flamenco dancer. As she was hanging round by the cake, dessert and confectionery counter, she kept stopping and pivoting slightly on the toes of her black high-heeled shoes to scan the tables.

When he made up his mind that it was she, he was once more overcome with the same apprehension he had almost shaken off with the effect of the cognacs he had drunk. After all, the reason they were meeting was to settle scores. They had come here for a reckoning. The young woman was going to get angry with him; maybe she would scream and shout. People were going to turn round and look at them. Seeing that there were places they could have met where no one knew him, where he knew that his friends and acquaintances would not show up, places that were out of sight, it had been a mistake to suggest this patisserie. But it was too late to think about that now. It was already done. She was a few steps away from him. She had already given up wandering around and was standing next to the large glass street door. She was looking at the people going in and out and glancing at her watch from time to time. Maybe she would wait a few minutes longer, and then leave. But then the feeling that she had been messed around and deceived would swell inside her. She would get even angrier. Not making it obvious that he was there, not showing himself was not an escape or a solution. She could easily find the address of the company he worked for when he was not writing. When he thought about days of agonized waiting for security to call, cold sweat ran down his back.

"There's a woman to see you, Bülent Bey," the security guard would say.

He did not even want to think about it. He got up and walked towards the door with slow steps.

"Hi!"

It came out of his mouth like a whisper.

The young woman smiled and reached out her hand: "Hi."

There was not the slightest sign of anger on her face or in her voice. Her calm allayed his fears.

"What would you like? Whisky? Cognac?"

"Could I have a tea, please," she said to the waiter who popped up next to them as they were sitting down, "with two slices of lemon?"

Then they began chatting about the Istanbul traffic, about the underground system that was always under construction, about the broken pavements . . . As the minutes passed, Bülent Serdar was on edge again. Whatever was going to happen had to happen now. The woman, though, was not taking any notice. She was flitting from topic to topic, without pausing for breath. At one point, she asked him how long he had been writing for the newspaper.

"Going on for three years. I used to write once a week, but now it's more often."

"You know, after reading your article, I began to buy that newspaper from time to time."

Then she stared into his eyes.

"What you wrote is right," she said. "You wrote the truth, but only up to a certain point. You made a mistake somewhere! You know how you called me a whore? Well, back then I wasn't. I only became one later. Slowly, I learned how to stomach it, think it, believe it, and I became one. Do you understand? Can you understand that?"

Her voice was velvety as she was saying this. There was no anger or hurt in it. It was as if she had sat down with one of her girlfriends and was talking about fashion, a new album or a meal she had had at a restaurant she had been to for the first time. Bülent Serdar's surprise showed on his face.

"But why are you looking at me like that, Bülent Bey? What is there to be surprised about? You didn't think I was going to shout and scream and make a scene here, did you?"

She stopped speaking for a moment and took a sip of her tea.

"Actually, I wanted to thank you. That's why I called you. That night in Mersin, I read your article over and over again. It moved me. I cried. How can I explain? It might seem strange to you, but you were the first person who thought about my life, about what I'd gone through and what I would go through, the first person who took me seriously. You know what, Bülent Bey? As a child, a teenager, and then later even as an adult, no one took me seriously. Oh, they always pretended to. They made it look as if they were. But my mum and dad, my boss, my friends, my lovers . . . None of them hung on my every word. They didn't want to.

"But I listened to everyone. First to my mum, my dad, my brothers . . . They'd tell me about problems I was already embroiled in, problems I was already going through, that I already knew. My friends, my lovers and the other men I was together with . . . They all thought that their own life was the most important thing. But what about my life? What about my problems? Were they really so completely unimportant? Didn't I have my own troubles and pain? But everyone kept dangling their own lives in front of me.

"That day when you left me in the middle of the road, I used to wonder if you remembered it. I did all the talking. You listened without interrupting. But will you still listen? Are you going to listen?"

How was he supposed to answer? What reply was he to give? It was as if she was setting off on a long journey and wanted to take him with her. Together they were going to set sail on unknown seas; they were going to cross bridges that had never been crossed before; they were going to break down doors that had never been opened before.

"But will you still listen? Are you going to listen?"

Listen meant share. She wanted to tell him things that she had not been able to tell anyone before, and share them with him. She expected him to be a witness to her life.

He flinched. He was thinking she might burden him with more than he could bear. But had he himself not prepared her for this journey by the very act of writing his article? Had he not stepped into her life and judged her? Even if it was a heavy burden, it was too late to shirk it now.

He looked into her eyes: "Would I have come here if I wasn't going to listen to you?" he said.

1

I woke up very early this morning. I stared at the white painted ceiling of the room for a while, listening to the calls of the seagulls coming in through the open window. Then my eyes drifted to my lover lying next to me. He was sleeping with his legs pulled up to his stomach and one of his arms under the pillow where his head was resting. I could hear him breathing. I got up silently. I took my nightgown from the foot of the bed, wrapped it round me and went out onto the balcony.

Whenever I met Orhan, we would come to this hotel in Bebek and we would always stay in the same room. I took a few deep breaths of that fresh Bosporus air. I cradled the back of my head in my hands and stretched. Then as I always did, I put my elbows on the iron balcony rail and watched the houses on the other side of the Bosporus as they were struck by the first rays of sunlight: Anadoluhisarı, the ferries going past leaving white foam in their wake, the fishing boats, the little motorboats . . .

I grew up breathing the Bosporus air. Our house was in one of the neighborhoods that had been built on the slopes behind the hills of Beykoz. We could smell the sea better on days when there was a southwest wind blowing. Even though we could not see it, we thought of ourselves as being of the Bosporus.

The summer I started the third year of primary school, I went down to Beykoz with my father one Sunday. We sat together in the tea garden on the quayside and drank Coke. I shall never forget it. We watched people fishing, children riding bikes, ferries going past. Then we had a long walk along the shore. I didn't let go of my father's hand the whole time. We walked past a pink house, its wooden shutters closed, set among trees with orange petunias dangling over its low garden walls; my father said, "I hope you'll have a house like that one day too."

That day, those words went in one of my child's ears and out the other, but in later years, who knows how many times I recalled them.

My father spent his life working, slaving away. He would get up early and leave the house while everyone was still asleep. He was a bricklayer. He worked with the same contractor for years. And six days a week, come rain or shine, he would always come back home tired in the evening darkness. He would flop down into an armchair and doze off. It used to be my job to wake him.

"Come on, my girl, the water's ready. It's time to get your father up!" my mother would say.

I would snuggle up next to him, stroke his hair and give him tiny kisses on the cheeks. I was used to the acrid smell of his sweat.

He would open his eyes a crack and say, "My little darling daughter." Then he would get up. We would go to the bathroom together. I would scoop out lukewarm water from the bucket with a blue plastic jug with a broken handle that my mother could never bring herself to throw out and pour it over his hands. He would soap up his hands and face, and then wipe his neck, behind his ears, his chest and shoulders with a cloth. When it was time for his feet, he would say, "You go now, my girl, I'll do my feet myself."

He was a very good man, my father. Later, whenever it occurred to me that I had not been home for a long time, I would chide myself for being so ungrateful.

My new life estranged me from my home and my neighborhood. When I bumped into anyone, they found my clothes, my makeup, and my way of speaking and acting strange. I was fed up with everyone looking but not saying or asking anything. I was fed up with my father telling me how much I'd changed each time.

I would make up stories and lie to them. I wanted them always to remember me as the old Zarife, as the little girl who poured water over her father's hands every evening. It was difficult for me to bring lies into my father's house, where my life ought to have been the truest and most uncomplicated.

Once, my mother was cutting potatoes in the kitchen. I was about to take the knife from her, but she looked at the black nail varnish I had on and said, "Leave it, dear, I'll see to it!" I felt so ashamed. She was such a stranger to well-kept, manicured hands and painted nails. During the meal, I couldn't work out what to do with my hands or how to hide them.

My family never used to ask me anything about my life. But I knew they were curious about it. They just didn't want to show it. We were playing a game with each other. But it wasn't easy for either side. Only Salih, my brother who was two years younger than me, wasn't part of it. Anyway, he'd moved out a while ago. But he was the one I was most wary of.

Ever since he was a boy, they'd called him "the bad penny". Even then, everyone understood that he lived in a different world with different dreams and that in the future he would have a different life.

He would read whatever he laid his hands on. He wanted to know everything, to learn everything. He would protest when he was wronged, he would fight back and continue arguing, scuffling and fighting to the bitter end. At school, his teachers adored him. He was top of all his classes. But he didn't shy away from games or football or the mischief children of his age get up to either.

I really like him and I respect him a lot. He passed his university entrance exams by working through the supplements in the newspapers. The same year, he started working with a customs broker in Karaköy. He graduated in economics, working and studying at the same time. Then he did his military service. When he came back, he married the daughter of the customs broker he worked with.

His wife Tuğçe is as beautiful as he is handsome. They're a good match; their life's so harmonious and well ordered. A while ago now, they moved to Selamiçeşme to be close to the architect's office where she works. They've got a four-roomed house on a street with lots of trees and greenery close to Bağdat Street.

Tuğçe's father offered to buy them a flat and furnish it, but Salih wouldn't hear of it. He's a young man who doesn't beg from anyone. For him life means resisting, fighting, struggling.

He told his father-in-law that they'd buy their own flat themselves and that he should let them stand on their own two feet. Tuğçe backed him up saying, "And that's why I love him." Seeing that they were both so determined, he made Salih a partner in his business instead.

The first time I went to visit them, Tuğçe showed me round the house. They had separate studies, each with their own computer. Noticing the shelves full of books on the walls of Salih's room, I said, "He's got so many books!"

"Yes, he reads every night. And I wouldn't have him any other way." Her eyes were gleaming as she said this. Her happiness made me happy too.

We went through to the living-room. She sat me down on what she told me was their most comfortable chair: a wicker chair with cushions next to a big window looking out onto the street with dark green plants lined up in front of it. We drank tea and ate some chocolate cake she had made the day before. She said that Salih was at a party meeting and that these days everyone had to do their bit and resist. She looked at the world through another window too, just like Salih did. The world they could see through that window was so alien to me.

It was the first time I'd been alone with Tuğçe. As I listened to what she said, I realized that I'd got her all wrong and that I'd filed her away in my head in a very different, very incorrect place. She was unaffected and straight as a die.

I already knew she had a wealthy family and that she'd gone to the French girls' high school in Harbiye and lived in Paris for a while. She had been born into that other world I longed for and dreamt of. She didn't have to do anything special or make any particular effort to live in that world. She was born lucky. She could buy whatever she wanted, she could wear whatever she wanted, she could go around and enjoy herself wherever she wanted. There were so many men with the same background as her that at first I just couldn't understand why she'd marry a boy from the slums like my brother who didn't have two halfpennies to rub together.

She said she didn't want a posh reception or a honeymoon. They got married in Şişli Registry Office one year ago. After they'd signed their names, she kissed her own father and mother's hands and cheeks, and then she gave my mother and father, my other brother and me a hug. "Now I'm your daughter and sister too." she said. She thanked us for "letting her have" Salih. My father struggled to hold back the tears.

That evening we all went for a meal at the Professors' Club in Baltalimanı as guests of one of Salih's teachers from university. He was an old man and he met us at the door. He shook all our hands.

As he kissed Tuğçe on the forehead, he said, "Take good care of your husband, my girl, he was my most brilliant student."

After dinner, he made a speech. He could not praise Salih enough. Tears welled up in our eyes as we listened . . .

"More cake?" Tuğçe asked. Without waiting for me to reply, she put a rather large slice down on my plate.

"Tell me a bit about Paris and what all you did there." I said.

"I'd been there once or twice before," she started, "but the last time I went I stayed for quite a long time. You know, I used to be in love with the place. With its streets, its buildings, its cafés, its people . . . Enough to want to live there for ever . . ."

She'd lived there for a year in a house that was close to a square named after an old prison, with a husband and wife who were teachers. She had made the most of that one year, wandering round the streets, buildings and cafés of Paris.

"Didn't you have any boyfriends there?" I asked.

"Of course!" she laughed. "But they were meaningless flings."

She said she'd briefly gone out with one or two young French men, but these relationships hadn't turned into unforgettable loves. She was not yet ready for love, not ready to fall in love.

"My feelings were focused on the city, on Paris itself. I was trying to find clues about my future there, and I did. That's where my idea about studying architecture was born. But I came back after a year when I understood that my heart was actually in my own city, in Istanbul," she said.

Once she returned, she shut herself up in the house and studied for the university entrance exams. She managed to get in to study architecture at Mimar Sinan University. From her first year there, she started to wander round the streets and squares again, but of Istanbul this time. She fetched a big box from her study. There were maybe thousands of photos inside. Streets, mosques, churches, arches, houses, doors, fountains, steps, roofs, columns, beams . . . She had taken all of them herself. She had scoured Istanbul, neighborhood by neighborhood, street by street, her camera round her neck.

"Salih and I are going to make a big book about Istanbul one day. It'll have lots of pictures. Salih will do the writing. You know, he's as besotted with this city as I am, but he looks at people and society and life more deeply than I do. He's better at grasping structures and transformations than I am. He has a way of looking at things that makes everything fall into place much more easily. So as you see, we complement each other," she said.

Her love for my brother and her belief in him really moved me. It didn't matter to her if you were wealthy or not, or if you were born in the slums or in a luxury apartment. But her idea of sharing her life with someone was not a run-of-the-mill, "who needs money when you've got love" type of relationship either. They had something far superior to this: theirs was a union where they looked at life from the same vantage point and saw the same things and thought the same things about what they could see.

But unfortunately, healthy life partnerships like theirs don't exist in the circles I moved in; there were no such pure and clean relationships. There never had been. Even what seemed to be the strongest relationship could suddenly come tumbling down like a house of cards with the smallest flick. People keep most relationships going by biting their tongues, turning a blind eye and burying their heads in the sand; people fool their partners and themselves . . .

She was surprised when I said I'd be going.

"Don't you want to see Salih? He'll be upset. We were going to eat together."

I didn't want to meet him.

"It's late, and I'm supposed to be going somewhere else, but I'll come again." I lied.

While going down the stairs, I muttered to myself, "No, I'm not ungrateful. Not at all . . . My problem's fear. Just fear . . ."

I could have had a life like Salih's too if I'd wanted. But I didn't. I'd found myself so many reasons, so many excuses not to want a life like that! You could hardly call me an unsuccessful student either. I didn't have to repeat any of my classes. When I got my high-school diploma, everyone congratulated me, Reşat Usta, the bricklayer's daughter.

I was a decent-looking girl and I blossomed early. By the last year of high school, I'd got to the point where I could no longer hide my swelling breasts beneath my school uniform. I used to get really fed up at men looking at me on the street and on the minibus as I went to and from school. I was very easily embarrassed back then. When my friends talked about boys, I wouldn't join in. I guess it was from me being a bit shy with my brothers, but I'd always keep my eyes on the ground when I was walking down the street.

Some of my friends would decorate their bedroom walls with pictures of singers they'd cut out of magazines, but I never had my own wall to put up pictures. At first, I slept in the same room as my brothers, but when I had my first period, they separated me from them. I always slept on the couch in the living-room after that. That's where I learned to resist sleep. They used to keep the TV on the whole day and only turn it off at night. I'd wait for a while after everyone had gone to bed, then I'd quietly get up and turn it on again. TV brought me those other, beautiful, colorful worlds. I used to watch films with happy endings. My greatest wish was to have a love like in those films. I would put myself in the place of the beautiful actresses: when they were sad, I would be sad; when they were happy, I would be happy.

There were erotic films on late at night. I would feel twinges in my loins as I watched naked men and women having sex in wide beds; something would stir inside me. Once, a young, handsome man started kissing the breasts of his lover, who was lying stark naked next to him in bed, and it was as if my nipples too began to tingle. I put my hands on my breasts and caressed my stiffening nipples through my flannel nightie. As I did, the twinges in my loins and the stirrings inside me became more intense. It was as if a secret power drew my hand further down. I shoved my fingers into my pants and started to let them wander between my legs. My whole body caught fire. Without taking my eyes off the naked man on the screen sucking the woman's nipples, I pressed my hand down on my vagina, which was secreting a sticky, warm liquid. There were pinpricks of sweat on my face. My body tensed up. When I came, it was all I could do not to cry out. From that night onwards, I started looking at men differently; I started looking at them with a woman's eye.

2

Quite a large boat with a mixed group on board drew up to the concrete quay on the waterfront next to the hotel. A young man who I imagined to be the captain from the hat he was wearing took two large trays—they were covered with shiny aluminum foil so I couldn't see what they had on them—, a large thermos and two plastic fold-up sun-loungers, all brought by an oldish woman. He put them by the deck rail. Then a young couple appeared on the quayside and got on the boat as their friends cheered.

Orhan had a boat too. He bought it the summer of the year we met. It would stay moored at the small quay in Bebek Cove. The next spring, we spent quite a few weekends together on it until we went off to Bodrum.

I was in love with Orhan back then. And he would tell me that he loved me and had tasted true happiness for the first time with me. I had a big romance with him in the beginning, but I knew from the first day that he had another life apart from his life with me. I managed to get over the unease of sharing the man I loved with another woman. I was able to do that. I was Orhan's girlfriend. My successful, wealthy, handsome lover who knew how to enjoy life offered me that colorful world I longed for and I wanted to make the most of it.

On a similar sunny morning, we too had docked at the quay, a little further down though, towards Arnavutköy, in front of the petrol station, and taken our friends on board. That Sunday was one of the happiest days I had with Orhan. He'd told me a week in advance that we'd be going out on the boat. That very day, I dashed off to Osmanbey in my lunch break and went to an expensive boutique on Halaskargazi Street that sold yachting clothes; I'd stop and look in the window every time I went past it. I bought some white shorts, a navy T-shirt, a pair of navy, rubber-soled canvas shoes and a bikini. The T-shirt had a small gold anchor embroidered on the breast pocket. I took what I'd bought back to the shop where I worked and hid them in my steel locker at the entrance to the warehouse because I wouldn't be able to take them home.

It was a real joy to cruise around on such a beautiful boat and play the hostess. I could barely contain myself the whole week. I waited impatiently for the weekend to come. We met on the Saturday evening. We had fish and rakı in the restaurant at the old Rumelihisarı ferry terminal. Orhan spent a long time talking about his work, as usual. It wasn't easy to run a huge factory with so many employees, to produce the goods the clients wanted, to do the marketing, to balance the books. But Orhan was hardworking and he could overcome every kind of difficulty. I gazed into his eyes as I listened to him over dinner. I hadn't seen him for one week. I'd missed him. I wanted to get up, put my arms round him, and smother him in kisses.

"You're tired. We can go if you like, darling," I said.

I knew it made him happy when I called him darling and asked about his health, his work or his problems. It was a happiness he hadn't had or been able to have at home in a very long time. He only felt it with me. We were together because I could give him this happiness. So what if he was married! What of it? What was the big deal? After all, isn't that what we call love? Suffering deep down inside for the person you love, shedding tears for them, making sacrifices for them without expecting anything in return and being consumed by them?

Orhan said, "Yes, let's go, sweetheart. You're right: I really am tired," and we got up to leave.

We got a taxi back to our hotel. We got undressed and went into the shower together. We dried each other with soft towels. Then we made love.

Day was just dawning when the wake-up call we'd requested the night before came. I got out of bed first. I had a shower, put on my new clothes and did my makeup. I looked at myself for a while in the full-length mirror on the wall and then went up to Orhan and sat on the bed next to him. I ran my fingers through his hair and stroked his face.

"Come on, darling, it's time to get up. We'll be late." I whispered in his ear.

He opened his eyes a crack. "Kiss me!" he said.

I leaned over and placed a kiss on his lips. "Come on; get up, my big baby. And straight into the bathroom!"

He used to act so childish and spoilt with me in the beginning. He had a shave and got dressed, and then put his hands on my shoulders and kissed me on the tip of my nose.

"You go down, babe. I'll be right there."

When I'd left the room, he closed the door behind me. I knew he was calling Izmir, his home. No matter what time it was, he would always phone home and talk to his wife every morning. He came down a few minutes later. We walked towards Bebek arm in arm. The sea was perfect. I got very excited as we approached the part of the cove where the boats were moored.

I'd been there a few times before when Orhan had just bought *The Queen* and was looking for someone to skipper her. I'd been round every nook and cranny of the three-cabined yacht. I'd been up on the bridge, taken the wheel and skippered her.

We saw Captain Recep, who was washing the little stern-mounted motorized lifeboat with seawater and his broom. He came down when he saw us and walked towards us. He dried his hands on a cloth he'd got stuffed into his belt and shook Orhan's hand and then mine.

"Welcome *beyim*. Welcome *hanımefendi*."

I was a hanımefendi when I was with Orhan. A hanımefendi before the age of twenty-three . . . How quickly everything can change in life! We climbed aboard. We sat down on the shiny, waterproof, off-white, faux leather seats at the rear. Captain Recep's deckhand Osman had laid on a lovely breakfast for us: butter, white cheese, honey, black olives sprinkled with thyme and chili pepper, peeled and sliced tomatoes and destalked green peppers . . . It was Orhan's lovely surprise for me. As we ate, he told me who would be coming with us, where we'd be calling in on and where we'd be having lunch. After we'd eaten our fill, Captain Recep started the engine. Once the yacht had left the shore and turned towards Arnavutköy at the mouth of the cove, we went up on the bridge.

There was a mixed group of ten or fifteen people gathered where we were going to dock. They started waving, shouting and whooping when they saw *The Queen*. We waved back at them. Then we disembarked and welcomed them on board.

It didn't take them long to get organized. Within a few minutes, *The Queen* set off for the opposite shore, the Anatolian side. To celebrate, his friends had brought a giant cake with "Happy Queen" written on it and six bottles of champagne in a big cooler. I didn't leave Orhan's side. We even cut the cake together. Drinks were poured, glasses were raised; we took our first sips amid shouts of "God bless her and all who sail in her! God save the Queen! Long live Orhan, Lord of the Seas!"

I was so happy I felt like I was flying. The yacht, the sea, the sun, the champagne, all the happy people . . . It was just like a film. At one point, Orhan leaned towards me and whispered in my ear to take care of our guests at the front of the boat.

I went up to the girls who were standing on the prow, talking and laughing among themselves. They were all young and pretty apart from one middle-aged woman who immediately attracted your attention because her lips were so thin, her face was so round and her hair was cut short like a man's. Orhan had introduced her to me as a famous designer. They were the girlfriends of the men on the yacht. They had all carefully chosen their clothes for the occasion. They were respectful and friendly to each other without a hint of jealousy in their eyes.

The men, though, were more of a mixed bunch. It was as if they were together in the same place by pure coincidence. They were handsome, ugly, paunchy, bald, mustachioed and clean-shaven and all around Orhan's age. The only thing they had in common was their wealth, which was reflected in how they spoke and behaved. Each one of them had a second life they shared with one of the girls and when I stood together among them too, my place in Orhan's life seemed even clearer to me.

As I was chatting with the girls, scenes from the Turkish films I used to watch suddenly appeared before my eyes. Because there were scenes like this in those films. Bad women called mistresses would enter the lives of happy couples. They would have dyed blonde hair, red-painted lips, false eyelashes and large hips. They would catch men in their webs and suck their blood like leeches. While their virtuous, pure and faithful wives were at home looking after the children, these bad women would be living it up at dances and balls or on yachts with their husbands. But none of these young, pretty girls on the boat was anything like those women I'd seen in films. There wasn't the slightest similarity. These girls weren't mistresses; they were cherished, loved, sought after, longed for, desired girlfriends. And they respected the wives of the men they were seeing. But who can go against nature and its laws? As long as there were men who had fallen prey to routine, monotony and the passage of time, these girlfriends would exist too. And if they didn't exist, there would have been others, other girls and women to enter those men's lives.

I caught sight of Füsun, who was telling something to the girls next to her. I'd known her since I first met Orhan. Her lover was one of Orhan's closest friends in Istanbul. He owned a big tourism company. Füsun had a pretty baby face and she had such a good figure that it could put the bodies of some of the most prominent models to shame. She had gone to a foreign language academy and now worked in the foreign exchange department of a bank and was earning quite well. She was roughly the same age as me. She was one of the few girls I wished I could be more like.

She met her lover a year ago in a bar in Çubuklu. He was very wealthy. There was nowhere in the world he hadn't visited. The things he told her made a big impression on her and they slept together the night they met. They saw each other frequently after that, but their relationship became more and more pained. He knew his wife had been cheating on him for years, but he nevertheless continued with the marriage. They'd sent their only son to America so he wouldn't have to witness their rows. He'd been studying at a university in Texas for two years. I saw a photo of him one evening when Orhan and I went to Füsun's house. He was handsome. As we were leaving, Füsun told me to call her, so we met in Teşvikiye the next day in a bar close to her house.

She was in a bad way.

She poured out her troubles to me: "Harun does to me whatever he can't get away with doing to his wife; he gets angry with her and takes it out on me."

Theirs was a difficult relationship to work out. He'd told her he trusted her more than he did his wife and had moved all the personal effects, documents, letters and photos he had in his house to Füsun's. When her two-room house in Koşuyolu was finally full to overflowing, he rented her quite a large apartment in Teşvikiye. Unfortunately, while the poor girl had dreamed her new house would be a love nest, everything turned into the opposite of what she had hoped for and expected. "I can hardly believe it myself, but on the nights his wife goes out, he comes to me, curls up at my feet and cries," she said.

In the early years of their marriage, Harun attributed his wife's insatiability in the bedroom, her hunger, her continual desire for sex to his own talent and ability. But it turned out that she was clinically addicted to sex. They say that there's no cure and it can only be kept under control with sex or with a barrage of drugs that dull the body. Harun found all this out long after he had transferred half of the shares in his company over to her. When it was too late, in other words. And that's when he started using happy powder. You know, cocaine gets all your energy going, it fans your sexual desire. It makes you more potent. He believed it was the only way he could keep his wife from straying, but it only made things worse for him. One night after he'd over-indulged in the white stuff, a blood vessel in his brain burst and he only narrowly avoided being paralyzed. The treatment he had after the operation had been of no use. But what good did it do him while he knew his wife was on her own, sleeping around in Istanbul, in luxury hotels, or on the south coast?

Now he'd started attacking the women around him as revenge. With all his money, which grew a little more each day, and his good looks, he had become one of the most popular men on the Istanbul party scene.

I was horrified by what Füsun told me. I couldn't imagine that nice refined man who had showered me with compliments when we first met curled up at her feet crying, even if she was his girlfriend. As we left the bar, Füsun said, "You know that boy whose photo you saw yesterday and you said how handsome he was, Harun's son? Well, he's gay. He turned out that way from all the resentment he's got for his mother and father. He's taking his revenge on them."

Where had these bad thoughts come from on that beautiful day when I should have been laughing and having fun? When I leaned over the railings and looked over to the back of the boat, I could see Orhan. He was holding a glass of champagne and talking to Harun.

"I'm glad Orhan's nothing like Harun. What would I have done if he was?" I sighed.

A big tanker was going past at that moment. *The Queen* rose and fell a few times as Captain Recep turned the prow into the waves so they come at us from the side. When the tanker had passed and all was clear again, I tried to work out where we were. I'd never looked at this shore and with its mansions and villas from here, from the sea before. Who knows how happy the people living there must be, I thought.

Then I thought about my father. I wondered what he was doing. I was sure he'd have got up early again. Whenever he was at home, he'd find himself something to do. And if he couldn't, he'd start removing the taps, descaling them and cleaning them with vinegar.

Do you know what it's like to spend years living without running water? They laid water pipes to within three houses of us, as far as Necmettin Amca's family—they were from my father's village—and stopped there. My father could never seem to come to an agreement with the local council.

First, they demanded he get planning permission! But who had planning permission in our neighborhood! And he never managed to put together the money to slip to the council workers. And no money meant no water. For years, we carried our water home from the tap in the mosque four streets away. We were one of only three houses in the whole neighborhood that hadn't been connected to the water supply. We would lug buckets full of water to fill the tank on the roof, but then the council told us to take the tank down. After much coming and going, and huffing and puffing, they finally called it quits with my father's second-hand radio cassette player and our water tank was allowed to stay.

I can't remember now which elections it was, but one evening two men we hadn't seen before came to our house. They told us to call the others over too, so the people from the other houses without water gathered at ours. They brought a Qur'an. Mothers, fathers, uncles and aunts all put their hands on it and promised to vote for them.

When they won the elections, they dug up our roads and laid pipes to our houses. I'll never forget the moment we heard the sweet sound of water flowing from our taps. My mother, my father, my brothers and me, we were all so happy. When we went into the bathroom, we didn't want to come out again the day the water came. I couldn't get enough of scrubbing and making myself clean. My mother told me my skin would peel off if I stayed in so long!

The Queen was in the waters opposite Paşabahçe. We were passing by a newly restored, large wooden residence and I couldn't work out if it was red or brown. The seafront patio was paved with white marble. In the corners next to the sea, there were sun loungers and small round tables with drinks glasses on them. I wondered which one was real life because if what I could see now was real, then what was the thing living a little further along the coast on the hills of Beykoz?

Which of them was real? If real life was further along the coast, in that neighborhood where the roads are untarred and houses flood with mud every time it rains and there are always power cuts, then what was what I could see before me?

It was after one o'clock when we arrived at Anadolukavağı. Orhan and I were the first to set foot on dry land. The fish restaurant was right next to the jetty and Orhan got them to set up two long tables side by side. Shepherd's salad, eggplant salad, white cheese, melon, hot paste, rocket and two big bottles of Yeni Rakı on each table . . . I guess you know that the sea air gives you an appetite. We attacked the meze as soon as we sat down. Before moving onto the hot starters—the calamari with *tarator* sauce, the pan-fried mussels, the fishcakes—Orhan stood up and thanked everyone for coming. I was sitting next to him in the middle of the long table in front of the window that looked out on the sea. As he was talking, he put his hand on my shoulder. That was a sign of how happy our relationship was. So I put my hand on his and laced my fingers between his fingers.

The steamed sea bass was brought out on round trays and everyone tucked in. Orhan was well respected and well liked in places like this. At the end of the meal, the restaurant owner, a young man, sent over big platters of fruit with sparklers on them. He came up to us and said, "These are on me, Orhan Bey." After we'd drunk our coffees and our liqueurs or cognacs, we left.

The first day I saw that young restaurant owner—I remember I couldn't work out why he'd let the nail of the little finger on his left hand grow so long. How could I have known that years later we might have been able to be together? How could I have known how well we'd get on? That I'd be able to contemplate a future with him? That I'd believe him when he told me he loved me? That I'd want to give myself to him because of that? That I'd sleep with him?

One day, he suddenly appeared in my life. After all that time, he called me and asked me how I was doing. Why had I given him my number? I always used to do that. One of us suggested meeting up and we met three times. He was fun, cheerful, knowledgeable and always had a lot to say. And single too . . . But he showed his true colors the third time we met.

We were in his house, sitting next to each other on a comfortable, burgundy velvet sofa, drinking our drinks and singing songs. He suddenly got up and went to the bathroom. He came back, sat down next to me again, put his little finger up to my nose and asked me to snort the white powder he'd got on his long nail.

I'd been avoiding herbs, powders and pills for a long time. I found people who used them to get their kicks and thrills and dreams and sexualities repellent. I was not the old Zarife any more. I was a successful businesswoman. I had my own money, my own house, my own car, my own life. I wasn't one of the chosen any more; I was one of the choosers. I did think of telling him where he could stick his powder, but I couldn't bring myself to do it.

He was actually a refined, well-informed and cultured man. And he had a very nice voice. What made him bring that powder and stick it up my nose? What the hell made him do it?

I had run out of hope once more.

3

As I raked up my past and strained my memory, I got confused. When was it? Four or was it five years ago? I don't know exactly. One hot July evening, we met up in one of the bars in Kalamış Marina with one of Orhan's old friends who he hadn't seen for a long time. He'd had a row with his wife and was staying on his boat, which was moored in the marina. He was smiley and cheerful. He told us in a loud voice about what he'd been doing and what all had happened to him in the past few months, mixing in witticisms and jokes. He was a nice man with his tanned skin, his hair that was greying towards his temples, his light-colored eyes and his athletic build. He'd bought a new villa in Dragos and that was what had started the row with his wife. The argument had dragged on for days. His wife, not to mention his two daughters, who didn't want to move away from their friends in Fenerbahçe, objected to the idea of moving to Dragos, and when neither side would back down things degenerated into a shouting match and a full-blown row. He hadn't seen his wife or children since.

Every time he paused while speaking, he would raise his glass and say, "Come on, down the hatch!" As we were counting, "one, two, three!", I lost track of how many whiskies I'd drunk, what with the music blaring out from the loudspeakers in the bar and trying to follow what he was saying without missing anything, and on top of that, the alcohol that was spreading through my veins. I was feeling very sluggish. He suggested we continue on the boat, so we got up and left.

We walked along the concrete wharf towards the pier. The cool wind that began to blow as night fell did me good. There were people sitting out on the rear decks of some of the boats we passed, drinking and speaking quietly so as not to disturb the people sleeping on neighboring boats. Orhan's friend's boat was a single-cabined, middle-sized motor yacht. You could tell from how clean its white paint was and how shiny its brass railings were that it was well looked after.

We took off our shoes next to the bollard the yacht was moored to. Orhan's friend got on the boat first. As we walked along the narrow wooden gangplank, which was fastened to the square stern with two big hooks, he reached out his hand and helped us aboard.

The rear deck was surprisingly large. In the middle, bamboo chairs were arranged around an oval table with a thick glass top. The cushions and the backs of the chairs were very soft. As Orhan and his friend were getting drinks ready on the wooden counter of the minibar to the right of the steps that went down to the cabin, I sat down and cradled the back of my head in my hands. The sea glistened in the moonlight and its tiny little waves had started to frolic with the wind. I was happy. I was living the life I wanted to live. It hadn't been easy for me to get out of my slum neighborhood. I thought about my friends from high school for a moment. Some of them had got bogged down with children and families, some of them had gone to university and scraped into jobs at banks and some of them had settled for being secretaries or working in shops. They had consumed their youth pining for very different lives.

"Only me . . ." I sighed, "I was the only one who managed to build a path to take me here."

"What was that? You were off in a world of your own."

"I was thinking," I replied.

Orhan's friend was understanding enough not to ask me what I was thinking about. No one asked anyone anything much in this life anyway. If you were telling someone something, you would only tell them as much as you wanted to tell. The first rules of this life were don't ask, don't pry and don't stick your nose in. You see, everyone had something to hide. The whole drama was acted out on a stage where the main roles were played by the men. People like me were just bit parts. We were supposed to look decorative and to help the lead actors take center stage and get more applause. They would do the talking and we would do the listening. They had never-ending and intractable problems. They would want us to share in them. That was the secret to being a girlfriend.

So you see, it was normal for him not to ask me what I was thinking. Orhan wouldn't have either. As far as he was concerned, there was no aspect of my life that was worth asking about. It would never have occurred to him that I might have my own problems that I wanted to talk about. Maybe he thought he made happy me with his wealth and just by being in my life, and that his wealth didn't leave any room for anything to be curious about in my life, that it prevented and would always prevent anything that might become a problem or that might be worth saying.

Most of the time we would just talk about trivial things. If I'm honest, I got fed up, not of Orhan himself, but of him always going back and repeating the same things. I knew every detail of his thirty-year marriage. It was hollowed out, meaningless, worn out, tired. I had no right to question, discuss or judge it. It was a taboo that no one apart from himself was allowed to touch. He too, just like all the other men, needed silent witnesses. But witnessing another life, learning about it, having to share it, even in silence, brings its own responsibilities. He would pour his heart out to me and then go off to

Izmir, to be with his wife, and I would be left alone with his problems that I had no right to question, discuss or judge. So I would swell with rage. I wanted to get my own back on him for being alone, for him leaving me on my own.

You know how you called me a whore? Well I actually chose to become one to get my revenge on him. No, don't you interrupt me! You're going to listen. You promised me. I became a whore to get back at him, to hurt him, to upset him. Maybe you're wondering if it worked. Well, it did. I'd be lying if I said it didn't. He got very upset at the beginning and did everything he could to try and stop me, but eventually he got used to it. I think him starting to notice how he also prostituted himself while he was trying to prevent me being a whore had a lot to do with it.

I'm assuming you don't think it only applies to women! This life, which is my choice, and which you too brush up against, however much you criticize it, however hard you try to avoid it, is essentially a cutthroat race to see who can out-whore the other. People will do anything to get one step ahead and cross the finishing line first. It makes no difference if the competitors are men or women.

I want you to think carefully before answering the question I'm about to ask. You're a journalist. Is everyone clean in your profession? Can you put your hand on your heart and say that? Without differentiating between men and women, in your own circle, among the people you refer to as colleagues, can you say that you've never witnessed anything whorish? What about not being able to write what you want to write, but pretending that you do, and thus deceiving your readers? What else can you call not being able to say that your boss won't let you and you're scared of losing your job and being left penniless? What else can you call deceiving people by flogging your dead horses? Isn't someone who sells their brain for material gain and then thinks and writes articles on behalf of the people who've bought his brain more of a whore than I am? I only sold my body; they sell their brains. I only harm myself, but who do they harm?

Anyway, where was I?

Ah yes, we continued drinking again on the boat. Orhan's friend was telling risqué jokes. We were laughing. In this life, you get to a point where you call a spade a spade. The conversation and laughter went round and came to the nocturnal exploits the two of them had had in European cities. They were telling each other what all they had done with women and how they'd fucked them.

At one point, Orhan got up to go down to the cabin and called his friend over as he went. I could imagine what they were doing down there. When his friend came back, he called me over: "Zarife, babe, could you come here a minute?"

I went down. I snorted a pinch of the white powder he offered me on a credit card with a tiny straw he'd made from the foil of a cigarette packet. I was an old hand at it. People in the bars and restaurants and on the boats I went to would offer each other cocaine, marijuana or pills like they were handing out cigarettes. They thought it was strange if you didn't snort, smoke, or pop. We went back up together.

Orhan explained at length how he'd taken a big-bottomed black Ghanaian woman from behind in a brothel in Frankfurt. She'd bent over the edge of the bed and let Orhan inside her.

Happy powder begins to have an effect on me very quickly. Whatever I listened to, heard, or thought before snorting it intensifies a hundred, a thousand times in my brain, in my body and between my legs. The same thing was happening again. I was turning into another woman as I listened to Orhan. After a while, I was no longer myself. I was now the most sought-after, the most desired, the most lusted-after woman of the sparkling nights, the bars and brothels of Frankfurt that I'd never been to and never seen.

Orhan said he was going downstairs. I went down after him. We grabbed each other and started to kiss madly. He undid my blouse. He was kissing my neck and trying to unhook my bra. I reached with my right hand down between his legs. He was hard. I knelt down and pressed my lips against his cock. I stayed like that for a while. I could feel it throbbing on my lips, like a heartbeat, through his trousers. I opened his belt and I hooked my thumbs inside the elastic of his pants and pulled them down together with his trousers. His cock sprung out like a bow. All of his muscles were tense. I pushed my forehead against his stomach and got him onto the bed. I pressed down on his trouser legs with one of my knees and he extricated his bare feet. He lay on his back on the bed and I got on top of him and knelt between his legs.

"Please, take me inside you," he begged.

I put my right thumb in his mouth. "Ssh! There's no point begging: it's not your night tonight!" I said.

Just then, I felt his friend's hands on my back. I knew he'd join us. I leaned forwards. He started kissing my bottom and between the cheeks. I pressed my chin down on Orhan's chest. He held my shoulders. Our eyes met. He wanted to say something. I put my thumb further into his mouth. He closed his eyes. His friend pushed up the skirt of that woman who wasn't me any more, pulled her panties down, grasped her hips with both hands and entered her.

But why are you blushing, Bülent Bey? You knew what kind woman you were coming here to meet. I'm telling you my life. If I don't tell you what happened as it happened, how will you understand me? If I wanted to, I could speak in a way that would spare your blushes and wouldn't force you to avert your eyes from me, but

I don't want to. I don't want to pick up some colored pens and jazz up some old photos of me. If you asked me if I'd like to go through those things again, I'd definitely say no. But I did go through them. It happened.

You can always tear up and throw away photos that remind you of a past you don't want to look at or you want to forget, Bülent Bey, but you can't be cleansed of your past. You can't be cleansed of those things on the photo just by tearing it up.

You gave me a chance when you agreed to meet with me, and I want to make the most of it. Let me, please.

4

It was already midday when I woke up. Orhan and his friend had both gone. I felt exhausted. When the powder wears off, you become sluggish and you reek. I had a hard time getting up. My clothes were scattered around the cabin. I picked them up, got dressed and went up on deck. The inside of my mouth was all furred. I sat down in a chair. I tried to down one of the bottles of water that was on the table, but I started retching as soon as the water reached my stomach. I leapt up and clung to the railings. I tried to be sick. My muscles tensed up; it felt as if I was about to bring up my entire stomach, but nothing came out apart from the few mouthfuls water I'd drunk. I wiped the sides of my mouth with a tissue. I felt twice as tired.

"What a dirty slut I am," I mumbled. "I'm disgusted with myself."

But it wasn't true. I knew very well what kind of night was waiting for me after all those stories of brothels, the alcohol I knocked back like water and the powder I snorted. I was ready for what was in store even before I went down to the cabin. Orhan's moans, him begging "baby", my screams, they were all a call to his friend. I wanted him to come down as quickly as possible. Just like every man, he too would later tell people somewhere that he'd shagged his friend's girlfriend, "on top of him, too". It excited me to think that Orhan would go down in the eyes of his friend, that he'd be humiliated. As I saw it, I was going to get my revenge on him for the similar nights he'd made me go through! But who was I kidding: sex was an area of freedom where Orhan went off the rails, you see. He had no limits. He thought of every woman apart from his wife as a toy he could toss aside once he'd had his fun and got bored. Besides, taboos are easily broken down where pills and powder are involved. That night too everything seemed to unfold so naturally. Revenge . . . It was an empty word. And before you ask, let me tell you: yes, I enjoyed myself a lot that night.

I mentioned similar nights. The first was in Antalya and the second was in Istanbul. One evening we went round for dinner to that woman who Orhan had told me was a famous designer on the boat trip I just told you about. Before dinner, we were going to look at some sketches of bags she'd prepared for him for the next season. He introduced me to her as being in the same line of work and a very good friend of his.

Sevinç was a smiley woman in spite of her masculine behavior, which I did find odd at first. She served us whisky in crystal glasses in the lounge. We each took a sip and then went through to the study. Her sketches were really good. Orhan chose five or six models, saying, "We can give them a go and see how they pan out."

Sevinç had done up her house very tastefully. We went back into the lounge, where a faint bluish white predominated. She'd used various shades of blue for the ceiling, the walls and the surfaces of the pouf chairs with their low backs and wide seats. There was a navy blue shag-pile carpet on the floor. The low coffee table, the side tables between the chairs and the large dining-table were topped with thick see-through glass. There were large, mainly red oil paintings on the walls; they gave color to the room and livened it up.

We had a French red wine with the meal. After a starter of onion soup, we each had two quails cooked in wine. Then Sevinç brought a single large piece of roast fillet steak to the table on a thick rectangular wooden board, like a chopping board. She carved it very skillfully and served us. The meal ended with tiramisu, which I was familiar with because I often went to Italian restaurants at that time.

Sevinç had been taking a very keen interest in me ever since we set foot through the door. Her eyes were on me throughout the meal. She was always talking to me. At one point, I felt overwhelmed by her looking into my eyes and bombarding me with questions all the time. After clearing the table, we went and sat in the lounge. I was filled with a sense of foreboding and I didn't know why. At first, I thought it was from the wine because whenever I have a bit too much, it gives me a headache and I feel uneasy; but this time, it wasn't the wine. There was something about the house that made me anxious. Although the furniture, the décor, the design and the hostess' hospitality should have made me feel at home, I was on edge. Sevinç put on a tango CD and left the room. Orhan, sitting opposite me, was flicking through a glossy magazine. She came back a short while later. She'd changed out of her poppy-red blouse and tight black trousers into a comfortable, loose, strappy, dark blue dress with small white dots on it. She was barefoot. She looked at me and, as if realizing that something was wrong, asked me if I had a headache.

She left the lounge before I could reply and came back with three tiny pills in the palm of her hand. "Take one of these, darling! Orhan, you take one too!" she said and gave us one each. She took one as well. No one said anything for a while. Orhan had gone back to his magazine. She sat with her legs folded on the chair next to him. She'd closed her eyes and was moving her head from side to side in time with the music. I got up and went over to the large sofa at the side so I could reach the nibbles on the coffee table more easily.

I felt I'd shaken off my unease and anxiety. I'd started to perk up.

About the same time, Sevinç practically leapt out of her chair and started to dance on her own in the middle of the room. Then she went up to Orhan and pulled him up by the hand. They began spinning together like lunatics in the middle of the lounge. The music had got louder too. I could hear the singer's voice, not just in my ears, but also in my hands, on my fingertips, in my feet and in my whole body now. When the rhythm of the music seemed to slow down, they calmed down as well. Orhan put his arms round Sevinç. They started kissing and couldn't keep their hands off each other. His were roving over her back, her hips, her bottom. At one time, I would have been jealous, but that phase was long past. Instead, I just leaned back on the sofa. I started to watch them while I sipped on my cognac as if I was at a private showing of a film.

Orhan was kissing Sevinç on the neck and shoulders. As I watched them, I started feeling aroused too. I put one of my hands onto my chest and I started to caress my erect nipples without making it obvious. At one point, Sevinç's eyes met mine. I jerked my hands away from my breasts. She smiled. Then she suddenly stopped and without taking her eyes off me, she said to Orhan, "Come on, let's strip, let's strip each other!"

At the same time, she started undoing the buttons on Orhan's shirt. In a few seconds, he was completely naked from the waist up. Then she came up to me, turned her back to me and told me to unzip her. Once the zip was open, she shook her dress off in a sudden movement. She was wearing nothing underneath.

The tangoes continued on the CD player. They started dancing again. They kept on spinning and kissing each other and as they were kissing, she would keep looking at me. There was something different about how she did it. It wasn't the sort of woman's glance I was used to. Our eyes met again. She smiled once more. Then she left Orhan and came and sat down next to me; she put her hand on my shoulder and pulled me towards her.

"You're very pretty, sweetheart. So very pretty," she said.

She kissed me on the lips. I didn't think of resisting, pulling away, or escaping. It was as if an electric current was flowing through me. I was tingling all over. It was like thousands of ants were crawling over my arms, my legs, my stomach . . . I let myself go and surrendered to her.

Orhan had disappeared. Sevinç slowly undressed me, stroking me, caressing me, teasing me . . . We said nothing to each other. I'd never been this close to a naked woman's body. I'd never tried, never thought about sex with a woman before, but at that moment, I wanted it. I wanted it a lot. Once I was completely naked, she laid me down on the sofa. She sat on the carpet on the floor, leaned over me and started kissing me, running her lips along my neck and on my breasts. She was caressing my legs, my stomach and between my legs with her hands. I closed my eyes. I gave tiny cries as she ran her hands and lips over my skin. That aroused her even more. She was breathing more rapidly.

"You drive me crazy, crazy . . ." she moaned, panting, "I can't take it any more . . ."

She got onto the sofa and lay on top of me so that my feet were by her face. She kissed my toes. Then she slowly moved backwards onto her knees. I could feel her hot breath between my legs. She brought her mouth very close and started to wander her tongue inside me. We came, our tongues inside each other, shuddering, moaning, crying out. We stayed like that for a time, interlaced.

It was almost morning when we left Sevinç's house. Orhan dropped me off in Ortaköy. I hadn't been there for a long time. I started to wander round the side streets by the seafront. None of the cafés, bars, restaurants and small gift shops had opened yet. I went down two more streets and came to the large square by the shore. It was completely deserted. I sat down in one of the wooden chairs belonging to the tea garden with two big plane trees in front of it. I felt drained, but it wasn't because of the tiredness of the night or not having slept. I'd had a row with Orhan in the car. Just as we were getting into the lift, he put on that sardonic air that always makes me angry and asked, "So how was it? Did you like it?"

When he couldn't get a reply out of me, he went on, "That's how pills make you crazy."

"I don't want to talk about it!" I snapped.

"Fine, we'll talk in the hotel."

"I'm not coming to the hotel; drop me off in Ortaköy," I said.

As I was sitting in the tea garden, the events of that night passed before my eyes. Would I have done the same things with a clear head? I was seized with a feeling of betrayal. I regretted this unusual night even though I might have been willing to experience it in other surroundings. Orhan had planned the whole thing and implemented it step by step. Designs for new bags, sketches and talking business were all part of his plan. He'd given me to that woman as a gift, wrapped me and presented me to her. Imagine it: being wrapped, offered and presented to someone . . . If I'd paid a bit more attention, I was sure I could have foreseen what was in store for me, but I didn't pay attention; or rather, I hadn't wanted to. Sevinç had made her intentions clear with her glances, her eyes that undressed me throughout the meal and her endless compliments. And I knew exactly what those tiny pills were. So why was I blaming Orhan? If being wrapped and given were my choice, why was I obsessing about having been offered? Why was it so difficult for me to accept what had happened?

I was the one who kept emphasizing how much of a whore I was in moments when I was fed up with my relationships and feeling helpless. The easiest way for someone to feel better about themselves is for them to demean themselves. I read that somewhere. Probably in Ahmet Altan.[1]

And I got used to thinking of myself as a whore before anyone else said it about me. Every time I repeated it, that's what I started to become. I would feel freer within my own smell, my own filth, my own habits. I'd found magic words, magic questions that I could resort to in moments when I felt I had to show that the incomprehensible was actually comprehensible, in situations when I believed I had to defend myself, and I'd feel better each time I resorted to them because they proved me right. "What's the big deal?" I kept asking, "What's the big fucking deal?"

The life I lived was my own choice. So what could have been more natural than to bear the consequences? Would Orhan and people like him have had a place in that other life, that old life of mine that I hadn't wanted, that I'd rejected and abandoned, in the lives of my family and Tuğçe and Salih? But I'd burned for the sort of life you can only have with Orhan and his kind. That was the life I was living. If that was being a whore, then I was a whore. After all, I was only behaving in the same way quite a few women who wanted to have this kind of life behaved. "What was the big deal? What was the big fucking deal?"

Anyway, weren't the men who lived this life whores too? Wasn't this life itself the very essence of whoredom?

A dog came up to my chair. It was a solemn dog with a huge head and a sorrowful look in its eyes. I stroked it.

---

1. Ahmet Altan: A popular Turkish novelist.

5

My friends and I used to go to Ortaköy a lot. We'd buy baked potatoes wrapped in tin foil with various fillings from the row of stands and we'd sit eating them in the same tea garden where I was pondering how much of a whore I was that morning. We were all young, we liked laughing and having fun, and we valued friendship. None of us were from rich families. We didn't have cars. We'd travel by bus, *dolmuş* minibus or ferry. We'd all dress in jeans, cheap shirts, blouses or T-shirts.

Ufuk was one of my friends. He lived in Kısıklı with his family. His father had been a petty officer and was an electronic technician by trade. After he retired, he started repairing TVs in their shop on Kısıklı Square. His mother was a housewife. After high school, Ufuk spent two years working in the accounts department of an export company; then he did his military service and continued working for the same company when he came back. He was also doing a correspondence course in management at the same time. He was twenty-five years old, medium tall, slightly stocky, fair skinned with blondish brown hair and a warm heart. We met on the boat from Üsküdar to Beşiktaş one spring morning; I'd been working in that leather shop in Mecidiyeköy for two years by then. We were sitting next to each other in one of the rows of seats out on deck. He dropped his lighter and as he was reaching for it, his elbow hit my arm and one or two

47

drops of his Coke splashed onto my dress. He went bright red and, apologizing profusely, offered me a tissue from his pocket. Then we introduced ourselves and chatted. When we got out, we walked up to the dolmuş stop together.

"See you around," he said as we parted.

The next morning, I found him waiting for me by the boat terminal. We sat next to each other again. We asked each other why we hadn't met before. Or maybe we had, but hadn't paid any attention in the morning stress we went through every day.

"There's nothing eye-catching or impressive about me, after all," he said.

"And there is about me?" I replied.

We were both just ordinary people, like most of the passengers. Ordinary people were only eye-catching when they got into fights, tripped over or got seasick on windy days and leaned over the guardrail on deck to throw up. Ufuk pointed out a girl who was sitting in the row of seats opposite us: "Or else you've got to be like her to get noticed!"

The girl he'd pointed out had interesting makeup. Her head, with its short black hair glistening and hardened with gel, reminded you of a hedgehog that had puffed out its spikes. She had a wide, bony forehead and had shaved off her eyebrows and traced a thin line with a black eyebrow pencil instead. She had dark green eye shadow on and she'd dyed her long eyelashes the same color as the bow-shaped lines she had instead of eyebrows. Her lipstick and the nail varnish on her short nails were the same brownish purplish color. She had four rings, each one of them different, in her left nostril. Everything she was wearing was dark black: from her knitted polo neck to her tight, pinwale corduroy trousers. She had combat boots with thick rubber soles on her feet and you could see the tops of her woolen socks. She had a silver cross hanging round her neck. I looked at her: she was dozing with her head resting on the shoulder of the young man with a ponytail and beard sitting next to her, and said, "If I dressed like that, my dad would throw me out."

We laughed.

"Do you think it's easy to be eye-catching?"

Back then, I had no problem with being ordinary.

6

Ufuk and I started waiting for each other at the boat terminal every morning. The friendship that had sprung up between us was more than being just ordinary travel companions. On the fourth day, he took me by my arm as we were walking towards the dolmuş stop in Beşiktaş and asked if we could meet that Sunday.

I'd known he would ask me this ever since I found him waiting for me at the terminal the day after we first met. I had the answer already prepared in my head: I was going to say yes. I was leaving behind the period when I could easily turn down a man who felt close to me for the sake of other men I'd never met, never known and had only dreamt about. I was twenty-two. Most of my friends from school and the people the same age as me in the neighborhood were already married.

Where I grew up, they took a very dim view of girls who weren't married by the age of twenty if they didn't go to university or if they weren't sick or disabled or didn't have a duty like tending their sick fathers or bedridden mothers. The matchmakers would come round once or twice to ask for your hand and then they'd never appear again. Gossip would start doing the rounds: "She must be loose," they'd say or, "Who knows where all she's been?" How cruel those always smiling women and those always sweet old ladies next door would become! All of a sudden, you were left completely defenseless! Ears would become deaf. Not being able to explain, the way they shunned you and didn't care, it really hurt.

The matchmakers came round to see me too. As far as my mother was concerned, they were good matches, but I found an excuse to get out of all of them. "He won't do; let's wait a bit longer," I'd say.

The last one was a distant relative. He was a thirty-five-year-old, fully trained mechanic. His father had sold off his house and land in the village and bought him a workshop in Çağlayan. He made good money. His mother and his sister had come knocking on our door three times. After my mother had nagged me on a few occasions just to take a look at him at the very least, I reluctantly agreed.

They came one Sunday with a huge bunch of flowers and a box of chocolates. He sat between his mother and his sister on the couch where I slept at night. I made them tea and served them. After they'd drunk it, his mother said to mine, "If it's okay with you, why don't the youngsters go out for a bit?"

We went in his car to Beylerbeyi and sat in the tea garden on the shore. Mustafa was serious; he didn't talk or laugh very much. If it wasn't for that bushy moustache on his top lip, you could even have called him handsome.

He told me he worked twelve or fourteen hours a day and that he'd been grappling with life since I was thirteen, but that thankfully he'd got somewhere with his hard work and effort. He had developed and expanded his business very quickly. He had five people working for him. Last year, he bought two flats, one on top of the other, in one of the side streets right at the beginning of the wide road in Mecidiyeköy that goes to Okmeydanı. He lived in the top flat with his mother, father and sister. As he was telling me this, he smiled shyly and said, "The bottom one's empty. It's waiting for its bride."

I looked away. When he saw that, he asked, "Have I done something wrong? Have I made you angry?"

"No, no . . . It's nothing. It's just I'm not used to this kind of conversation," I stammered.

My reply made him feel better. He said he'd taken a detour to and from work a few times and passed by the shop I work in. He'd seen me and he liked me. He wanted to get married and start a family.

"I love children. A boy or a girl, it's not important; it's enough that they're good, hardworking and honest," he said.

He himself hadn't studied, but he was definitely going to make sure his children did: "Studying and learning means understanding and knowing life, and I'd like my children to understand and know life. That's how they should live. A good mother is a teacher: she teaches her children what's right and beautiful. Wouldn't you agree, Zarife Hanım?" Then he looked into my eyes and said in an emotional voice, "Who knows how good a mother you'd make? Think about it, please think about it. I'll wait."

We got up. He said nothing more about it on the way back. When we got home, my mother heard the sound of the car and came out. She wanted to invite him in.

"Thanks *teyze*, but it's late," he said. "Tell my mum and sister and we'll be off."

His mother gave me a hug at the door and kissed me on the cheeks saying, "Come round to ours too, my girl, and bring your mum along as well. Our house is your house. We are relatives, after all."

As they were leaving, Mustafa and I shook hands.

"See you soon, Zarife Hanım," he said in a soft voice.

"See you soon, Mustafa Bey."

Once they'd gone, I told my mother I was just going to pop round to Şükran's for half an hour and went out. Şükran and her family lived one street behind us. I popped in to see her for five minutes so I wouldn't have lied to my mother and then I walked to the bottom end of the neighborhood, towards where the orchards started. I wanted some time alone to collect my thoughts and listen to myself.

Mustafa had been very respectful and understanding. He said what he meant and meant what he said. He was one of those men who quite a few girls I knew wouldn't be able to find no matter how hard they tried. As I was listening to him, I had read in his eyes the decisiveness of those who really believe what they're saying, but was that enough for me to be his wife?

He'd said I'd make a good mother. Could I really be a good mother and bring up good children? Would I be able to manage it? Would I be able to cope? I'd overheard his sister in the kitchen telling my mother that her brother's wife wouldn't have to work. Mustafa's wife would be the lady of the house.

It sounded very nice, but still, was it what I really wanted? To be a good wife, a good mother, the lady of the house . . . But in the end wasn't that just being like my mother? She too was a very good wife and a very good mother, but she wasn't living the sort of life that I longed for and that I wanted to live. She couldn't. But I was expected to opt for a life like hers. Do you think it's easy to choose? Do you think it's easy to say yes to a life you've never longed for or dreamed of? If Mustafa had appeared three years ago, when I was sitting around at home bored out of my skull, maybe I could have said yes to this good match that came knocking at my door.

I'd been working for three years and I had an okay income. My father had opposed it at first; he wouldn't have his daughter working. My mother and I ganged up and had a hard time convincing him. Then he put his foot down about not taking his daughter's money.

So I was secretly giving my mother part of my salary. I'd learned how to make do with what I had at an early age. As for clothes, what do you think the local factory shops, seamstresses and dressmakers are for? In the shop, we immediately heard about which factories were selling off surpluses, where there were going to be end-of-line sales and which warehouses stock came to. You should have seen what all I carted home for my mother, my father and my brothers for two years. They would get so happy when they saw me at the door with plastic bags in my hands.

If after all was said and done being Mustafa Usta the mechanic's wife meant being like Reşat Usta the bricklayer's wife, what difference would it make if I moved from my father's house to my husband's house? Maybe I'd live a little better and a little more comfortably, maybe money wouldn't be as tight as before, but was that enough to say yes to Mustafa?

"You'll get used to him and learn to love him!" Şükran said.

Really? What if I couldn't? Then what would happen then to those dreams I had on the couch at night? Looking into each other's eyes, holding hands, embracing, making love? What would happen to them?

Like all husbands, Mustafa too would ask me if I loved him. What could I say? If I didn't love him, if I'd never loved him and hadn't been able to love him, was I supposed to lie to him? This new life of mine that I didn't want, that I'd never thought about, that had been foisted upon me, forced upon me, was I supposed to build it on a lie? Can you be a good wife or a good mother in a life fuelled by lies? Is it possible?

"I won't be able to do it, mum. It won't work. Go and tell them I'm not ready to get married. Just tell them something. Mustafa might be a good person, but it won't work. I can't do it," I said.

"Okay, love," said my mother. "Okay, I'll go and tell them." The subject was never broached again at home.

7

"Aren't you going to say anything? How many times have I asked you now? Or haven't you been listening to me?" asked Ufuk.

I looked at him. "Sorry, I was miles away . . . We can meet on Sunday? That should be fine, but can I tell you for sure tomorrow morning?"

After we said good-bye, I walked briskly towards the bus stop at the start of Barbaros Boulevard. The stop seemed more crowded than usual that morning.

"I'd be better off getting the minibus up to Zincirlikuyu and then taking a taxi from there," I thought to myself, "or else I'll be late for work."

I spent three or four hours of my day traveling to and from work and I was well and truly sick of buses, minibuses and crowds. I only liked the ten-minute boat journey. Not just in spring and summer, but even on those cold winter days when it got dark early . . . I'd close my eyes and listen to the sound of the waves. On stormy days when I was getting on and off the boat, it would rock and as droplets of seawater would wet my face, I'd imagine it was dark and I was on a rickety boat buffeted by the furious waves on a rough sea. There were no stars in the sky. The moon would appear and then disappear again from between large dark clouds. I'd stand ramrod straight for hours at the prow of the wooden boat cleaving through the giant foaming waves without the slightest feeling of fear or fatigue. I'd get wet, sopping wet. Water would trickle down from the ends of my hair, from my shoulders, from my fingertips . . . The long, white dress I was wearing would cling to my body like a second skin. The water that washed over me and flowed off in all directions would caress my bare feet. I must have traveled countless on this sea in this boat. As the darkness in the sky dissipated, the sea too would slowly begin to calm. It would turn blue again in the sun. At first, my island would appear like a dot, and then it would begin to get bigger and take on form and color in the middle of the endless blue. I'd jump in and glide through the water towards the shore. Behind me, I'd hear the sound of the boat departing for other seas and other journeys. Then nothing, apart from the leaves rustling and the birds singing. I'd get undressed and stretch out on the cool, damp sands. As the sun rose, the sand would begin to warm up and get hot and so would my naked body. I'd feel the heat of the sun on my drying lips and nipples the most. I'd close my eyes and set off for the realm of dreams . . .

I got out of the minibus in Zincirlikuyu. I crossed the road and hailed a taxi.

"Mecidiyeköy," I said, "I know it's only two stops away, but . . ."

The driver interrupted me, saying, "No problem, love. I'm hardly going to leave you stranded here just because you're not going very far, am I?"

I looked at my watch when I got out in front of the shop. It wasn't nine o'clock yet. I took a look inside. Not a soul.

"Why on earth am I always in such a hurry?" I sighed.

I headed for the side door. I said hello to the person on the information desk and took the lift to the third floor to the accounts department. The people there started work an hour earlier than we did. I got the keys from the accounts manager's secretary and went downstairs.

I opened the shop. It was actually Rifat Bey who was supposed to open up. He'd been sent to us as to be the shop manager a year ago and we later discovered he was the boss's brother-in-law. He had come on time and opened up once or twice in the beginning, but then he got all of us together one morning and asked which one of us had been there the longest. I said I had, so he turned to me and said that from now on, I'd be opening the shop in the morning. And from that day, it was always me who opened up.

At first, this new duty seemed like an extra burden, but in the weeks to come, it gave me a privileged position in the company. Giving me the keys to a shop where there were goods worth billions of lira was proof of how much they trusted me. Our boss always had to pop in early in the morning before any of his many business trips and I was the only person he ever saw. One day, he called me into his office when he came back from a trip to Ankara.

"When does that brother-in-law of mine actually come to work, for God's sake?" he asked. The only thing he could do was to turn a blind eye: he didn't want to upset his wife just because of her little brother's irresponsibility. And with my help, he was going to put up with him for as long as it took. He called after me just as I was going out the door, "It's down to you, my girl. You'll be the one running the shop!"

At the beginning of the next month, I got a far bigger raise than I'd been hoping for. From that day on, I made a point of not coming in late and I always tried to get to the shop early. As the months went on, we never saw Rifat Bey. The other shop assistants and the errand boys would ask me if they had any questions about work. And now I was the one who took care of stock entries, sales lists and cashing up. Once I had a bit of money in my pocket and was rid of the cheap sweatshirts I used to wear, I'd become an attractive businesswoman with my hairdo and manicure. My family took a different view of me now too. My mother would just call me "my girl" and words like marriage or matchmaker were banished from the house. How strange this thing called money was! You might not be able to buy love with it, but you could definitely buy understanding, respect, and freedom . . .

That's why it was so easy for me to tell Ufuk that meeting him that Sunday would be fine. The money I pressed into my mother's hand each month was more than what my father made. We'd got a new dining-table, a new iron and an oven and we'd replaced quite a few other little things round the house that had seen better days. We never spoke about it, but couldn't my father see all this? Where had that bike for my youngest brother come from? Where had Salih got those new football boots he was wearing from? Even as proud a man as Reşat Usta the bricklayer could stomach some things when he had to.

What were they going to say if I told them I was going out on Sunday? What could they say? They ought to have realized that me going regularly to and from work six days a week and spending Sundays at home would eventually change. They should have understood that I got bored being the only girl in the house on those crowded, noisy Sundays with the whole family and that the incessant gossip in the neighborhood, the reproaches and the criticism suffocated me. There were other things in life for me to experience apart from trying to feel in my own body the sex I saw on a muted TV set at night on the couch, or lying stark naked on the sands of imaginary islands, waiting for men who didn't exist.

For quite a long time, I'd been pulling my blanket up over my head as soon as I got into bed, closing my eyes and trying to fall asleep quickly. I'd read in a magazine that women who were used to touching themselves and satisfying their sexual appetites themselves when they were young wouldn't be happy with men in the future. I couldn't, wouldn't ask anyone if this article was true or not, but after reading it, I didn't put my hand between my legs again. I was afraid. It would be almost unbearable some nights, but I'd immediately stop and link my hands behind my head and try to sleep like that. If I wouldn't be able to make my man happy in the future, if me caressing and stroking myself, making love to myself would prevent me being happy tomorrow, I could stop, even if it was difficult and almost unbearable. I had to stop. If I wasn't going to be able to offer my body as a sacred gift to the man I'd fall in love with and marry one day, then what would be the point of me abstaining and jealously guarding it?

Around that time, the desert-island dreams I had on the boat became more frequent and intense. I didn't want them to be like the nocturnal sex I watched on TV. As soon as I could feel my nipples becoming hard and something stirring in my loins, I'd open my eyes and everything would abruptly end . . .

My mother didn't ask me anything when I told her I'd be going out with friends that Sunday. She only told me not to be too late back or else they'd get worried.

My father had recently turned into someone who didn't say very much and didn't ask many questions. He'd always be the last to know about anything happening at home, but I made sure he was in earshot when I told my mother I'd be going out on Sunday. I wanted to test him and see what his reaction would be, but he just bowed his head and said nothing. It was painful to see him so quiet, so helpless and at such a loss for words.

I realized I'd upset him and got annoyed with myself, but what the hell was I expecting the poor man to say? "Well done, my darling girl's grown up and she's going out"? What was he supposed to say? What else could he do apart from getting upset?

I couldn't take my eyes off him, sitting there motionless in his chair, his head bowed. He looked so old, but he wasn't even forty-five. His once jet-black hair had gone completely white in the last year or two. His cheeks had become hollow. Dark rings had appeared round his eyes. He used to laugh and chat, and joke and play with his kids. What had happened to make him suddenly crumble like this? He didn't say anything any more when he came home in the evening. When pressed, he'd bring the conversation to an end by saying, "What's there to tell about a building site? It's just dust and soil." Then he'd stare off into space and stay like that.

He'd broken off all his ties with the world apart from work and home. He didn't read the paper or watch TV. He used to make my brothers angry—they were both mad about Fenerbahçe—with his Galatasaray hat, he used to wrestle and grapple with them, he used to be glued to the radio on Sundays when the football started, but now he didn't ask who'd won or who'd lost, not even in the important matches. He had no interest in anything. It was as if his life had reached a certain point and then frozen.

At first, my mother objected and wanted to resist this change and draw him back to life, but when she saw that her efforts were all for nothing, she lost hope and gave up. After a while, I stopped asking him or consulting him about anything any more, just like my brothers did. Our father was there and not there for us. We still respected and loved him as before. But you could feel the same respect and love for a father who'd died. And our father was no different from any father who'd died. I don't think dying necessarily means when your soul leaves your body and they put you in the ground. You can be dead while you're still alive too. If life means having dreams, imagining the future and longing for tomorrow, then our father was already dead. Once you lose hope and have no more branches to cling to, life no longer has any meaning. One day you begin not knowing what you're living for. You're spent. Getting annoyed or angry can also be a way to grab hold of a part of life again, but he had forgotten how to do that. He'd definitely heard I'd be going out on Sunday, but he didn't get annoyed or angry. He didn't say anything. He was so far away from life that he couldn't get angry or annoyed. Perhaps he deliberately shrank away from life to keep his pride undented and his honor intact so he wouldn't have to submit and stomach things and run away from things he didn't like. I've no idea.

Would I end up like my father one day too? This question suddenly seemed to seize my mind. I immediately banished it. No, I wasn't going to be like him. I wasn't going to die while I was still alive. I had a job I loved. I had a mother, brothers and friends who loved me. I had hopes, dreams and longings. I loved life. I'd started looking at the world differently. I was seeing and feeling things I never used to see or feel and they bound me to life much more strongly than ever before. The change in my job had transformed the way I looked at life. I'd taken a step up and even though it was only one step, life seemed different. I still had a lot of steps to go . . .

"I told my family. We can meet on Sunday," I said.

Ufuk's eyes lit up: "So you managed to get permission. I can't tell you how pleased I am." As he was saying this, he took my hand in his and held it there for a while. Those few seconds seemed like long minutes that wouldn't pass. I was worried about what to do if anyone saw us, but at the same time, I was anxious not to give him the impression I was completely inexperienced. I was all confused.

"I'm really pleased too," I said as I pulled my hand away.

On the boat, we talked about what time we'd meet on Sunday morning, where we'd go and what we'd do.

We met at the boat terminal in Üsküdar towards noon on Sunday. I found Ufuk looking at magazines in front of the snack bar there.

I crept up behind him silently and tapped him on the shoulder. He jumped. He had a red long-stemmed rose in his hand.

"For you," he said.

It was the first flower I ever got from a man. I paused for a moment and then sniffed it, guessing that was the right thing to do. "Thank you," I said, "it's very kind of you."

When we got to Beşiktaş, Ufuk hailed a taxi. We went up to Taksim and walked past the Republic Memorial towards İstiklal Street. It was very crowded. The sound of people talking, shouting and laughing mingled with the noise coming from the music shops and turned into to an almighty din.

As we went past the McDonald's on the corner of Küçükparmakkapı Street, he asked me if I'd like a hamburger. He took me by the arm and pulled me towards the door without waiting for me to reply. It was full of mixed groups of young people. When I saw them, I was suddenly free from that fear that someone might see us that I'd felt when he took my hand in his in Üsküdar. While we were queuing up by the tills, he stood behind me and put his hands round my waist; I leaned back lightly on his chest as I wasn't hiding from anyone any more.

After our hamburgers, we went to see a Julia Roberts film. When the lights went off, he leaned over towards me and with the tips of his fingers started stroking my right hand, which was over the armrest between our seats. It was a feeling I'd never had before. I got very excited. My palm was drenched in sweat, but I kept it there because I was afraid those touches and caresses might end.

After the cinema, we walked hand in hand down the street to the Çiçek Pasajı, where we met Ufuk's friends, who were sitting at one of the tables outside a *meyhane* called Kime Ne. They looked like a cheerful lot and they raised their beer glasses when they saw us approaching hand in hand and shouted welcome. While Ufuk was saying hello to his friends, I stood shyly next to the table. A girl with a cute face noticed and called me over: "Come, sit next to me. Ufuk will come and sit on the other side of you in a moment," she said.

That's how I met Burçin. She was very chatty. She barely paused for breath as she told me that she hadn't gone to university after leaving school; she'd had one or two jobs and had been working in Yeşilköy Airport for the past few months in the customs clearance office of the same company as Ufuk, but what she really wanted was to work in one of the duty-free shops in the international terminal. She said she had one or two friends working there. They'd found ways of making a decent amount of extra cash by selling the perfumes, cigarettes and alcohol they'd bought duty-free outside with a rather hefty mark-up. She was chatty and pretty. I immediately took to her.

As soon as Ufuk sat down next to me, he flung his right arm round my shoulder with a sense of ease that he got from being with his friends. I'd experienced quite a few firsts one after the other that day: it was the first time I'd gone out with a man, the first time I'd got flowers from a man, the first time I'd gone to the cinema with a man and the first time I'd held hands with a man. It was the happiest day of my life. When Ufuk was talking to me, he didn't use my name; he kept calling me things like darling, babe and sweetheart. That evening, after our first kiss, he started calling me his one true love. Love . . . Is there any better word to describe it when two people complement each other, become "one", are "true"?

I had a lot of fun in Çiçek Pasajı that day. Because I wasn't used to alcohol, my muscles relaxed and my head started to spin after the second beer. I leaned my head on Ufuk's shoulder. I'd started seeing him differently. That shy, quiet, retiring youth from the boat had gone, and in his place was a self-confident man who knew what he was talking about and made you listen to what he was saying. I'd made the right decision when I agreed to go out with him. Now I too had private things to tell my friends, instead of just telling them what was happening in the shop in Mecidiyeköy: I had a boyfriend I could show off and boast about.

We left as it was getting dark and walked hand in hand again up to Taksim. Then we got a taxi to Beşiktaş. I didn't want that beautiful day to end; I wanted the happiness I was feeling to last forever. As the boat drew up alongside the terminal in Üsküdar, Ufuk asked me if I wanted to go for a little walk. I said yes without hesitating.

We walked towards Kuzguncuk. At one point, he wanted to take my arm, but I said not here and pushed his arm away. I realized he was upset and asked him if he was angry with me. He smiled: "Why should I be? It was me who was in the wrong!"

We were going past the Tekel factory in Paşalimanı. There was no one else around. I snuggled up to him and took his arm. I could feel his warmth in my own body. My insides, my heart, my blood were all nice and warm.

"You know, something stirred inside me the first moment I saw you on the boat. I really fancied you and I was scared I wouldn't see you again," he said.

"You were scared? Really?"

"Yes, very."

I snuggled up a bit closer.

"And I thought you'd never take a step, give a sign or, I don't know, make a move," I said, "but today I'm so happy. Please don't be cross with me for pushing your arm away just now. I've never had a boyfriend before. I've experienced so many things with you today that I'd never experienced before that my head's all in a spin. Forgive me."

Before I could finish what I was saying, he took my face in his hands, pulled it towards him and kissed me on the lips. Just at that moment, the driver of a car going past beeped his horn and we panicked like naughty children caught in the act. We started running along the pavement as if someone was chasing after us. When we got to the corner of the Tekel building, Ufuk said, "Let's turn off here," and we found ourselves in the park by the shore.

There wasn't a soul in the park either. We were out of breath from running. We sat down on the first bench we saw. In front of us was the sea and the Istanbul skyline stood opposite us like a lit-up tableau. Without saying anything, we watched it for a while. It was as if we were afraid of making eye contact or speaking.

"It's all just like a film," I sighed. On the way here, Ufuk said he was scared he wouldn't see me again. And two steps later, he held my face in his hands and kissed me on the lips and then we escaped hand in hand! I'd seen similar scenes in countless films. If people didn't go through these things in real life, would they have made those films? But for some reason, they always had unhappy endings. Jealous people or bad guys would come between the star-crossed lovers and separate them. Gossip, envy, lies, slander . . . There was nothing the lovers could do about it. They'd suffer, they'd shed tears and in the end they'd submit. After many trials, everything would finally come to light, but by the time black turned to white and desperation turned to hope, they would unfortunately have reached the end of the road from which there was no turning back. They would go to death together to show the world how great was their regret and how exalted was the love they had lost and found again, to prove that not even death could separate them . . .

But having said that, there were films with happy endings as well. Films that showed joy, excitement and happiness in nice lives that I wanted to have too.

A restless excitement that I'd never felt before spread through me.

No one we knew would do anything bad to us. I'd met Ufuk's closest friends: Kemal, İlhan, Burçin and the others . . . They were all kind, sincere and good people. And I didn't have any close friends apart from Şükran, who has a heart of gold. She whooped with joy when I told her I was going to go out with Ufuk. I knew my mother and brothers would like him when they got to know him, and his family would like me; they'd take me under their wing and call me their daughter.

A brand new period in my life was beginning. I didn't have to dream my desert-island dreams on the boat any more; I didn't have to put myself in the place of the women having sex on screen in those long nights in front of the TV.

"You were miles away, darling."

He put his arms around me.

"I was thinking about us. I'm so happy, darling."

We started to kiss. My body caught fire as he unbuttoned my blouse. I closed my eyes and waited for him to undo my bra. At that moment, my heart started to beat so hard I thought it was going to leap out. I felt like I was going to go mad with pleasure as he caressed and kissed my breasts. No one had ever seen or touched them before. I bit my lips so I wouldn't cry out or scream. We said I love you to each other maybe a hundred times.

Everyone had already long since gone to bed by the time I got home. For the first time in months, I didn't turn on the TV. My mother had got my bed ready. I got undressed silently, slipped into bed and immediately closed my eyes.

8

Before I came here, I thought a lot about whether me telling my life story right down to the smallest detail to someone I'd never seen or met before, a stranger, was the right thing to do. My mind kept coming back to the word "stranger", so I repeated it out loud a few times: "stranger, stranger, stranger". Then I decided I would tell everything. If being a stranger—I said to myself—means not knowing someone, not knowing what they're thinking, just being satisfied with as much as they tell you and not being curious about the reasons and consequences of what they tell you, then who wasn't a stranger to me? Who? My family? My friends? My boyfriends?

Ufuk aside, you're the only person who's ever taken an interest in my life, Bülent Bey. You're the only person who's ever taken me seriously. Even though I might not agree with everything you think of me, I still find you're much closer to me than other people who've come into my life, who are around me, who've never known anything other than the life they live. That's why it's so important that you vouch for me.

Ufuk was my first love, and I've never loved anyone so much. I feel a pang every time I remember him.

After that first session in that park in Paşalimanı, we spent some very happy, beautiful days together. We'd meet up every Sunday. In the whole of Istanbul, there was no park we hadn't strolled through, no street we hadn't wandered down, no tea garden we hadn't sat in. We told each other the most beautiful words that can ever be said; we gave each other the biggest hopes that can be given. We were going to join hands and have a life we'd bedeck with the most beautiful colors the world had to offer. Our life would be full of love and happiness. Together, we would lay its foundations; together, we would carry its building blocks; together, we would build its walls. Lies, deceit, unfaithfulness and betrayal would have no place in our world. That was the type of life we had both wished for before we ever met. We had both been waiting for someone we could share that kind of life with. Our wishes and dreams came true when we met each other.

As I'd been expecting, when my mother and my brothers met Ufuk, they took to him immediately. Every time he came round, my mother wouldn't leave him alone: she would force-feed him her *gözleme* with poppy seeds and cheese and her *kol böreği*, telling him she'd made them specially for him and wouldn't take no for an answer.

Even my father, who never spoke, would find his tongue when he saw him. Ufuk knew how to be an adult among adults and a child among children.

I got very excited one Wednesday when he said, "You're coming round to ours this Sunday; my family are expecting you." For four whole days, I could barely contain myself. I stopped eating and drinking. All I could think of was what I'd wear, how I'd behave with his mother and father, and what all I'd talk about that day. One lunchtime, I went to a shop in Kağıthane where they sold end-of-line clothes and bought a skirt suit that made me look more feminine. As I was trying it on in front of the mirror, I thought I looked like an elegant and beautiful businesswoman I'd seen on TV in an advert for a hair dye. She also wore a grey suit like this as she shuttled back and forth between airports, clutching her patent leather briefcase. When we finally met in Üsküdar on Sunday afternoon, Ufuk couldn't believe his eyes when he saw me.

"You're completely transformed; you look so elegant," he said.

"I think I've gone a bit over the top," I sighed.

He was wearing a casual shirt and his usual navy trousers.

"I can't take you on the bus or the dolmuş wearing that," he said.

We got a taxi to Kısıklı.

Ufuk's family lived in a two-story stone house with a garden. They'd inherited it from his grandfather. Halide Hanım, his mother, met us at the gate. She was short, rather plump, smiley and chatty. She gave me a hug and kissed me on the cheeks before Ufuk had the chance to introduce us and said, "Welcome, my girl, you're really very pretty."

I could feel myself blushing as I said, "Thank you, *teyzeciğim.*"

Their sitting-room was on the ground floor and looked out onto the garden. When I bent down to take my shoes off as I was going in, she told me that they didn't take their shoes off on that floor.

Halide Hanım had a way with words that won you over and made you warm to her. Ufuk left us alone in the sitting-room to chat about things that are of more interest to women and went upstairs, to his father. About half an hour later, Halide Hanım was going to make some coffee and called them down from the bottom of stairs.

Lütfü Bey, Ufuk's father, was tall, burly and healthy-looking. He had a deep, mellow voice. Both of Ufuk's parents spoke pure clean Istanbul Turkish. Their families had been in Istanbul for several generations. They were polite and measured. I really liked the way he always prefaced what he was saying to me with "*Hanımkızım*" because I wasn't really used to hearing words like that where I lived. They didn't ask me anything about my family or my life apart from one or two general questions like, "How are your mother and father, and your brothers? Are they well?"

Ufuk was an only child. His mother and father had only words of praise for his hard-working spirit and honesty. I felt proud of him as I listened to them. When Halide Hanım headed for the door saying, "I wonder if the *börek* is done yet", I got up as well.

"Let me give you a hand, teyzeciğim," I said.

We went to the kitchen together. I poured out the tea while Halide Hanım cut the *su böreği* she took from the oven into slices.

"You know, my girl," she said, "it's got to the point where recently you're all Ufuk talks about at home. He likes you a lot and we like you too. I hope your friendship blossoms."

"Thank you, teyzeciğim," I said. "I really like Ufuk as well."

We had börek, tea and chatted. The time flew by. As I was leaving, Halide Hanım and Lütfü Bey saw me off saying, "Our lovely girl, *hanımkızımız*, come back and visit us again soon."

Ufuk and I left the house together. As he was seeing me on to the Beykoz dolmuş in Üsküdar, he said, "My family really liked you. I can't tell you how happy I am."

He waited at the stop until my minibus set off. Then he waved after me. At dinner, I told my mother and father and my brothers everything down to the smallest details: all about Halide Hanım, Lütfü Bey, what we talked about, the house they lived in, the su böreği we ate and even the taste of the tea we drank. After dinner, I went to Şükran's and repeated everything I'd told my family to her as well.

That night I had a charmed sleep.

9

Then everything suddenly changed. How did I make, how could I have made that decision that tore me away from my family, from the people I knew and from the values I'd known to be right since my childhood? I haven't been able to find a plausible, satisfying answer yet, even though I've asked myself many times. At first, I blamed Burçin, but I knew even then that I was being unfair on her. She was only a spark that fell on the dried grasslands inside me. How had the people around me neglected for so long to notice that I had dried out inside and turned into grasslands that could catch fire at any moment? This transformation must have been reflected in my speech and behavior. How could they not have seen it? Your speech, behavior and personality don't just change overnight, do they?

The things I lived through back then pass before my eyes like a film now . . .

One Sunday when I went to Ortaköy to have baked potatoes with Ufuk and his friends, Burçin said, "One day why don't we meet up just the two of us, girl-to-girl, what do you say?" While I was thinking of a reply, Ufuk stepped in and said, "Yes, why don't you two meet up from time to time?" So we decided to meet in a café in Teşvikiye three days later.

It was round about then that Burçin had quit her job and started work at one of the duty-free shops in Yeşilköy Airport where she'd wanted to work for some time. Wednesday was her day off because she worked at the weekend too.

She was as trim and elegant as she was pretty. Her makeup, manicure, clothes and accessories made her immediately stand out among our friends. Because I didn't really know Teşvikiye, it was she who suggested we could meet in a café called Zanzibar. It was inside a big passage. When I walked in, I found her sitting at a table next to the window with a glass of wine in front of her. I was wearing the grey skirt suit I'd worn to go and see Ufuk's family. When she saw me, she stood up and kissed me on the cheeks saying, "You're beautiful anyway, but you're so much more beautiful when you take a bit of care of yourself, darling."

The place wasn't like anywhere I'd ever been to or seen before. Everything was different: from the starched white table-cloths to what the waiters were wearing, from the names of the food on the menu to the shapes of the glasses. At every table there were men and women, all of them wearing expensive clothes and all of them elegant.

To get there, I'd got out of the bus at Osmanbey and walked down Rumeli Street, passing by its boutiques, shoe shops and gift shops. Everything cost a fortune here. I stood outside a few shops and looked at the customers inside. They could comfortably pay more money than I earned in a month for a skirt and blouse or for a pair of Italian shoes. I envied the women walking down the street carrying flashy bags from the shops they'd been to.

This was another Istanbul and I didn't belong here at all. It was very different from Beykoz, Üsküdar, Kısıklı or Çağlayan. There were two types of people here: the ones who belonged and the ones who were here to serve the ones who belonged. Concierges, waiters, servants, low-paid shop assistants, small shopkeepers, drivers . . . There were people like us, in other words, and there were the rich.

I almost bumped into an old man on the footpath. He was coming out of a shop carrying some bags. He immediately set them down, lightly held me by the arm and apologized. He was tall and handsome with blue eyes. At that moment, I visualized my father's prematurely wrinkled face, his grey hair, his sunken shoulders and his rough, cracked hands. My father, like my mother and brothers, had never set foot here. They lived another life in another world, on the hills of Beykoz. They muddled through, suffering all the while. Their happinesses and joys, their problems and pains belonged to that tiny life, just as they did.

I suddenly remembered Salih watching what was on TV one dinnertime and telling me, "Everyone gets the life they deserve, *abla*." Then he continued, "But you yourself have to decide what you deserve." And when my father replied, "But there's no two people the same in this world, son!" Salih got angry and left the table.

Ever since he was little, he'd always been a hardworking lad who took what he could get; he rebelled against every kind of injustice and always believed he was in the right. If he was faced with three paths all going to the same place, he'd choose the steepest, hardest one.

When he was at university, he came home one day with a sheaf of manifestoes. My father was very worried: "You'll get us into all sorts of bother," he said. Salih replied defiantly, "I don't want to be herded like a sheep, dad. I want to live like a human being, but you can't do that without putting up a fight."

But I didn't see life in the same way; I didn't think of it on the same terms. I was happy with my lot. I had a family who loved me and a place I could call home. My boss and the people I worked with in the shop liked me. Although it wasn't officially my job title, in a short time I'd risen to become shop manager. My boss had given me a generous raise. When I met Ufuk, my hopes for the future blossomed and my self-confidence grew. My life had become interesting: I'd met new people and made new friends.

I was telling Burçin all this and I expected she'd share my happiness, but she asked me, "And is that enough for you, sweetheart? You only come to this world once; you only live once. Do we have to make do just with whatever life offers us on a plate? Can't we ask for more? Can't we ask for something better, something more beautiful?"

I didn't know what to say. I'd heard Salih say similar things too quite a few times, but his starting point and the method he wanted to use to get a better, more beautiful life were very different to Burçin's. As far as she was concerned, once you'd opted for a better, more beautiful life and decided you were going to live that life, the rest was simple.

"First of all, we should be able to escape from our shadow, or at the very least, we should try!" she used to say.

She believed that if we wanted to change our custom and tradition-smothered lives, we first had to tear out whatever in our lives was old and worn. The old values that kept us so restricted, that forced us to think and rethink every step we took were only good for making our lives similar to our mothers'. "How will we become free," she asked, "how will we escape if we can't break these rules that constrict our lives? If we can't throw out these old, out-of-date values that keep us in thrall to a life we don't want? If we can't overcome the obstacles put in front of us in the name of custom and tradition?"

I'd never thought of asking myself these things before; I'd never thought of questioning my life from this angle. The more I listened, the more I agreed with her. And anyway, wanting to live a better, more beautiful life didn't mean turning my back on my family and the people I loved. If I could manage do it, my mother, father and brothers could share in my new life. I could make sure that they too had a happier, more comfortable way of life.

"We should talk about this more often," she said as we were leaving Zanzibar.

As my friendship with Burçin deepened, my life changed too. We'd meet in a café or bar in Teşvikiye, Maçka or Nişantaşı after work on Wednesdays, when she was free. She always seemed to be wearing something more elegant than the last time I saw her. "You start changing yourself by changing your outward appearance," she would say.

And after a while, I started copying her. Clothes really do make a difference: the more elegant I became, the more my self-confidence grew. No matter how posh the places we went to were, I no longer felt like an outsider. No one thought I was out of place.

"And what would madam like today?" the waiters would ask.

"A gin and tonic, with lots of ice, please," I'd reply.

We'd sometimes sit on the high stools at the bar and chat with the barman or the customers next to us. People came to these kinds of places to have a nice time, to have a laugh and to have fun. You left your worries, cares and problems at the door. People would tell each other jokes, talk about funny things that had happened and keep each other entertained. Life and the world both seemed very beautiful when viewed from places like these.

I had a lot of fun when I was with Ufuk's friends too. Burçin couldn't join us because she had to work at weekends. I thought they might be curious about what all she was doing, so once or twice, I tried talking to them about her, but none of them was interested. Only later I understood that their lack of interest, to me incomprehensible, was because that sense of belonging that comes from sharing a similar life had disappeared. They simply didn't think of her as one of them any longer.

Ufuk had already told me he wanted to marry me. He said he'd get me an engagement ring in the third year of his correspondence course and we'd get married once he'd graduated, and that we were practically betrothed anyway, so we decided to save ourselves for our wedding night. We did all the sexual things you can do without losing your virginity. I'd got over my initial embarrassment. At first, I'd been reluctant even to touch his penis, but now I'd take it in my hand, stroke it and kiss it. In our encounters, I also began to understand how important getting hard and coming are for a man. From when he began to get hard until the moment he came, he was my captive, my slave. Knowing this gave me a lot of pleasure. To prolong it as much as possible, I performed the love games on him I'd learned from the girls I'd seen in the films on TV. When he was about to come, first his body would tense up like a bow and then it would begin to quiver and shudder. And after he'd come, he'd turn into an innocent child that needs to be stroked and caressed. I'd stroke his face and his hair and then push his head between my legs, and he'd make me feel the same quivering and shuddering.

Unfortunately, though, we couldn't be alone as often as we wanted. We didn't have a place of our own. We tried to have some fun in Ufuk's house one Sunday when his parents had gone to visit relatives in Fatih, but it didn't work. We didn't even dare take our clothes off for fear that they might come back early. If you're wondering why we didn't try any of the tourist hotels, we didn't have enough money, so out of desperation, we'd go round to visit Ufuk's friends. They knew why we were there, so they'd make their excuses and leave their house to us for a few hours.

One time I met up with Burçin, she said that sexual frustration lead to all sorts of mental problems in women. "Thank God I don't have that sort of problem!" I said.

We only talked about Ufuk that day. She knew him very well

because they'd worked together for about a year. "He's a very good person," she was saying, "a real gentleman, very hardworking and reliable too, but he looks at the future through such a narrow window."

Ufuk really had taken his father's simple life as a model for himself: he made do with what he had and wasn't driven to get more. The thought of staying at the same company and getting promoted to supervisor and then to manager once he'd finished his correspondence course and got his management diploma, and the raises he would get was enough to make him happy. Because he was an only child, the house in Kısıklı and the shop in the market were both thought of as being his in a way. He didn't want any more than that. Oh, and he was going to buy a car when we got married.

After he introduced me to his family, he started the custom of us all eating together in their house. We'd go to Kısıklı almost every Sunday. In spite of all Halide Hanım's and Lütfü Bey's friendliness and kindness, I didn't want to share the only day that belonged to me and Ufuk with them. But I couldn't say anything to him in case he got upset and thought worse of me.

With Burçin as my guide, I had nudged open the door of those other lives and Ufuk's life began to pale in comparison. Every time we met, he'd go on about his work and his lessons, but it didn't occur to him that I also had a life worth being curious about. Once when I was about to tell him about the places I went to with Burçin, he cut me off in mid-sentence saying, "They're not our sort of place."

I often asked myself why things that had made me happy until recently didn't no longer made me happy, but I couldn't find an answer. Burçin told me I was in a different place now and that was why: "When the place you're in changes, your longings and dreams change too, just like the things you can see. If you really love Ufuk, you can still change him, open new windows for him and show him things he can't see, but first you yourself have to see, get to know and experience the things you want to show him; you have to feel like you're a part of that life you long for."

When we said good-bye that day, we agreed to meet up in Akmerkez next time.

10

I'd been to Akmerkez before: once with Şükran and once with a girl from work. As you know, it isn't just a place for only people with money in their pockets. Even if they can't buy anything from the luxury shops there, young people from the slums who want to breathe the same air as their wealthy counterparts go there too. They're the staff at the joints selling hamburgers, *döner* and pizza on the top floor on Saturdays and Sundays.

Anyway, one Sunday I went there with Şükran. I was in the last year of high school. I knew my mother wouldn't let us go into the center of Istanbul alone, so I lied and said I was going to study at a friend's house.

When we passed through the security check on the door and stepped inside, the gleaming shop windows, the expensive luxury products on sale, the elegance of the crowd of men and women and the bright colors made us feel giddy. You'll never understand what all the light, glitz and color meant to girls like us from the slums. You'll never understand if you weren't born into a room lit by a single light bulb. The evenings of my childhood and teenage years were illuminated with forty-watt bulbs that turned everything sallow, but it wasn't only the lights and the colors; the shop windows fascinated me too. They contained everything I'd seen in adverts on TV and in glossy magazines, everything I'd longed for, everything I'd filled my first teenage dreams with.

After milling around for a bit, we took the escalator up to the top floor; we melted into the crowd of young people and sat down in one of the eateries. We only had enough money for one bag of fries each.

"Life just isn't fair. God has opened different doors for everyone," I said to Şükran.

"But you've got the chance to get your foot in other doors," she replied.

Şükran had had to leave school in the first year of high school because her mother was ill and this had really upset her. That's why she'd get so happy about my success in school and that day she was as happy as if it was she who'd be taking the university entrance exams in a few months.

"Girl," she said, "with your brains, you'll end up as a lawyer before five years are up, and then the doors of the shops downstairs will open for you too."

There was a grain of truth in what she said. I'd got all the way through high school without a hitch. Neither my lessons nor the university entrance exams held any fear for me. With a bit of effort, I could easily get in to do something like law, economics or literature. But I gave up studying after high school. Maybe I was tired of it or maybe I wanted to have my own money as soon as I could. I don't know. It just felt so much better when I started earning some money, even though it wasn't very much, and could spend it how I wanted.

The second time I went to Akmerkez, I went into a sportswear shop and bought myself a denim suit with silver embroidery on the back of the jacket and the back pockets of the trousers. My friend from work said, "All that money for that? You could have got the same thing much cheaper in Kağıthane."

"They're not the same thing!" I snapped.

Wandering from factory to factory and from warehouse to warehouse looking for tat was not the same thing as shopping like a lady in a luxury shop in Akmerkez. If she'd pressed me a little more, I'd have told her how as a child my feet used to get swollen from wandering from stall to stall in Salıpazarı or Beykoz market holding my mother's hand just to buy a poxy little skirt or a cotton T-shirt . . . That for as long as I could remember, I'd never been able to buy anything I wanted . . . That my mother's and father's faces would fall every time someone mentioned money . . . And that I was sick, sore and tired of struggling to make ends meet. Luckily though, she just said, "Maybe you're right," and shut up.

I was going to meet Burçin on the bottom floor, in the restaurant in Homestore. I followed the directions the person on the information desk at the door had given me and found it easily. I sat at the table the waiter pointed to and ordered a glass of red wine. Until just a few months ago, it would never even have occurred to me to set foot through the door of somewhere like this, let alone sit down and have a glass of wine. "How quickly people change," I said to myself.

As I was watching the people sitting at nearby tables or coming and going, I realized that most of them had light skin and light-brown or blond hair. In my neighborhood, in the school I went to and in the place I worked though, everyone had dark skin and black hair. As I was looking around, I suddenly remembered the day Şükran and I came here and had some fries on the top floor. Most of the young people we saw there that day had dark skin and black hair too, but it wasn't just their coloring; their clothes and their behavior made them different to the people I saw in Homestore as well. As I was thinking about this, a voice from above me asked, "Would you mind if I join you, madam?"

I looked up. I knew the face before me from somewhere.

"I guess you don't recognize me," he said as he reached out his hand, "Orhan . . . From Izmir."

Then I remembered where I knew him from. I told him my name too as I was shaking his hand. Orhan Bey had a leather factory in Izmir. My boss would buy lots of things like bags, wallets and belts from him. We'd bumped into each other a few times outside the shop.

He sat down on the chair opposite me without waiting for me to reply. He was tall, handsome and tanned. He must have been close to fifty. There were a few grey hairs in his thick, dark chestnut hair. He smiled as he talked and there were small wrinkles next to his eyes.

"Were you waiting for someone?" he asked.

"Yes, a friend . . ." I replied and so as not to cause any misunder-standings, I immediately added, ". . . a girlfriend."

He seemed relieved to hear that.

"To tell you the truth, I didn't recognize you at first. You've changed so much!" he said.

I blushed and my palms started sweating because I wasn't used to hearing things like this from men I didn't know, but I quickly regained my composure. "We've got a right to let our hair down once a week too," I said.

Then we spent a while talking about the fluctuations in the leather market, his new business contacts in Germany and Belgium, and exchange rates. He was chatty. He flitted from one subject to another. In the space of fifteen minutes, he'd mentioned all sorts of things: the special discount he'd given on the last batch of handbags he'd sent to our shop, the drinks in the bar of the hotel he stays at when he comes to Istanbul, how his children were doing at school and the boat he'd just placed an order for. When he'd been round the houses and was back to handbags, Burçin had arrived and sat down next to us.

"We can get some food now, seeing your friend's here," said Orhan Bey.

As I was thinking about how to react to this unexpected suggestion, Burçin intervened and said, "Thank you very much, Orhan Bey, but, please, you order for us."

We each had cream of tomato soup to start followed by filet mignon (a name I couldn't get my mouth round back then) with lots of mushrooms. The three glasses of full-bodied red wine that I drank one after the other were making my head spin. Orhan Bey paid the bill and got up without waiting for us to finish the Italian coffees we'd ordered. He kissed us both on the cheeks as he left.

"That Orhan Bey's very sweet," said Burçin. I said nothing, so she added, "You see, it's those kinds of friendships that will add color to your life, darling."

Then, we had a little argument about my silence during the meal. Burçin said, "The man makes time for us, invites us to eat and you don't open your mouth to say a single word!"

"What have I got to talk about with a man old enough to be my father?" I replied.

According to her, there were quite a few advantages to being friends with experienced, mature men. Every man was a teacher. "We shouldn't be stupid enough to spend our whole lives with the first man who pops up in front of us, like our mothers did," she said.

"And what about Ufuk?" I asked.

He was the first man who'd popped up in front of me. He loved me enough to think of getting married. But there was a grain of truth in what Burçin was saying too, and I'd read similar things in various magazines. One of the main reasons why lots of marriages didn't work was that people got married without knowing the opposite sex well. Because young married couples were inexperienced, they would start to grow and look at life differently once the honeymoon period was over. After a while, this would lead to personality clashes.

As I was thinking about all this, there was a question gnawing away my mind: Should I tell Ufuk I'd had a meal with Orhan Bey? How would he react when he heard I'd had food and wine with a strange man? When I asked Burçin, she said, "Are you crazy, sweetheart? You can't go round saying things like that!"

I met up with her almost every Wednesday for three months. The way she behaved and spoke had an effect on me. She had strengths that I lacked, like self-confidence, decisiveness and cheek. She was relaxed when she was talking to Orhan Bey, as if she had known him for years, but I still blushed when I talked to men in the shop where I worked.

"How can you be so relaxed with an older man you've never met before?" I asked.

"It's a long story . . ." she said. She saw that I was curious, so she started to tell me: "I used to be like you at first too . . ."

The year after she left high school, she had several boyfriends while she was studying French literature at Yıldız University. That one year that she spent at university played a big part in her growing out of her former immature behavior, but the real change happened when she got to know men who were quite a lot older and more experienced than she was.

She lived in Kadıköy. One day while she and a girlfriend were waiting at the bus stop at the entrance to the Bosporus Bridge, a car with an Edirne number plate pulled up in front of them and the woman driving asked them an address in Kadıköy. As they were trying to give directions, the woman realized that they lived on the other side. "Seeing we're going in the same direction, I'll drop you off," she said and they got into the car.

Since then, Burçin had "got into the whole hitchhiking thing", as she put it. She started doing it, sometimes with a friend and some-times alone, at the start of the slip road leading to the bridge two or three times a week. At first, she was quite nervous about getting into cars driven by men she didn't know, but she soon got used to it. Because there was a lot of traffic on the bridge at the times she was going across, the drivers who were inching along were glad to pick up someone they could have a conversation with. On these short journeys, she met many men from all walks of life and with every kind of per-sonality: married and single, young and old . . . She'd been asked out on dates or for meals by more men than she could remember and she'd had brief relationships with one of two that she liked.

"Fine, but was there never anyone who tried it on?" I asked.

Apparently not.

"And it wasn't like I was obliged to get into every car that stopped for me. When you look into a man's eyes, you can tell what's going through his mind. So there's nothing to be scared of," she said.

Someone she met hitchhiking helped her get her job in the duty-free shop too. He worked for the national airline and managed to sort things out for her with a single phone call. She had dinner with him the same week to return the favor. They went to a fish restaurant in Kireçburnu. For the whole meal, he bared his soul to her, telling her he'd been married for thirty years, was fed up with his wife, and could no longer bear to see her face.

"Burçin Hanım, you make me feel young again. I hope this won't be the last time we meet," he said.

The second time they met, he gave her an expensive necklace and she let him kiss her on the lips.

"You mean, you let someone you didn't know from Adam kiss you on the lips?" I asked.

"What's the big deal? Do you think a kiss is going to wear out my lips?" she laughed.

I didn't know what to say.

First, Orhan Bey comes and sits at our table and then Burçin tells me all this. I was totally confused. My own life was monotonous. Burçin had a much more exciting and colorful life than I did, but that wasn't enough for her: she dreamt of another life that she believed would make her even happier. Even though she couldn't quite put her finger on it and couldn't quite work out all the details in her head, she was doing everything she could to make her dreams come true.

During the meal, she said, "If everyone's going to be satisfied with what there already is and what they already have and with what they're given, how can the world go forward?" and Orhan Bey had agreed with her. Successful people were always those who weren't satisfied with what there already was and who wanted more. Their lives were more beautiful and colorful, richer and happier than the lives of either my or Ufuk's family. The more I spoke with Burçin, the more I seemed to see the limits of the future Ufuk and I would build together and how that future would trap me. There was no place for grand shop windows, bright shiny colors, stylish clothes, nice restaurants or early evenings in bars full of cheery people in that future. No matter how hard we tried as a couple, we would always be mere spectators of those other lives.

11

The next week, I went to take some new designs for bags to one of our customers on Yıldız Hill. As I was coming out of their office, I got caught in the rain, so I took shelter under an overhang and waited for it to stop. When it did, instead of going down to Beşiktaş, it was as if an invisible force was compelling me to walk up Barbaros Boulevard towards the slip road for the Bosporus Bridge. It started pouring again about the time I got to the start of it, so I waved at a passing car. It stopped a few meters further along.

Do you remember, Bülent Bey? You were driving. You lowered your window and said, "Yes?" And I asked you if you were going to the other side. It was a stupid question. "Where else do you think I could be going to from here?" you answered. "If you're getting in, then please be quick about it. Let's not have the people behind swearing at us!" you said and I hopped in.

You didn't seem particularly talkative. When we went round the corner and you saw the long queue of traffic ahead, you said to me, "Since we're traveling companions, you could at least say something. I'm a journalist, so you never know, you might give me some material for an article."

I drew courage from your gentle voice and your politeness, so I told you about my family and my job. I told you about my brothers. You took an interest in what I was saying, but once we were over the bridge and at the tollbooths, you asked me where you should drop me off. I suddenly felt that I hadn't been able to explain the things I wanted to tell you fully.

"Wherever you want," I said.

I saw that you were surprised, so I decided to play at being Burçin and added, "You can even take me out to dinner if you like."

You looked at me with incomprehension.

"What's the big deal?" I said. "It's only dinner."

Then, again like Burçin, I did my best to talk about seizing the most beautiful parts of life, about living and going on without looking back, about being ready to pay the price for the life you long for, if necessary. But it had no effect on you. You dropped me off at the Kızıltoprak exit.

I walked towards the main street. It had started to drizzle again. I clung to the iron grille in the wall of a small cemetery that was on my way and cried my eyes out. I felt such a sense of betrayal. I couldn't accept that you'd just driven off without listening to what I'd wanted to tell you and left me like a forlorn kitten in the middle of the road. I'd had enough of people pretending to listen. At first, you acted as if you were interested in what I was telling you too—you even asked me questions—but then you left me and drove off without giving me the chance to say what I wanted to say. Acting and speaking like Burçin had done me no good.

At that time, I was at a crossroads: my head was full of hundreds of questions I didn't know the answers to. I really needed someone with whom I could discuss my problems, ask questions and share what was going through my mind, someone who'd listen to me without trying to give me advice or protect me, without judging me. I was taken in by the gentleness in your voice and clung to you like a lifebelt, but you let me down badly that day. After you'd gone, I kept wondering if you'd have let Burçin out of your car too if it had been her instead of me.

I couldn't help it, and I didn't want to be, but I was jealous of her. I asked myself what she had that made her any better than me. Looks? I was as beautiful as her. More so even when I was wearing something good . . . But clearly, looks weren't enough. At Homestore, when my eyes met Orhan Bey's for a moment, I got flustered. If Burçin was better than me because she didn't get flustered when men looked at her and met their glances with a womanly twinkle in her eye, then the first thing I had to do was to be more of a woman, I thought.

That day, on the strength of what Burçin had told me, I went and stood at the slip road going to the bridge. The invisible force was just an excuse I made up to settle my nerves. If I didn't envy that twinkle Burçin had in her eye, would the invisible force, which I'd never felt before, have entered me and compelled me like it did?

As I was getting on the dolmuş in Kızıltoprak, I consoled myself that I was still in one piece in spite of everything and that I'd succeed next time.

But I couldn't. I was never able to pluck up the courage to hitch-hike ever again.

12

I went back in when I heard Orhan calling, "When did you get up, babe?" He was in bed with his arms wide open, waiting for me. "Come, sit down next to me," he said. I perched on the edge of the bed saying, "I guess you're up again."

I started stroking his cock through the bedspread. I knew he'd sulk, grumble, and generally ruin my day if I didn't give him any attention. Orhan comes quickly. We must have done it hundreds of times, but he's never once been able to get off in the normal way. He always needs there to be something kinky or perverted for him to be happy. At least on nights when he's had too much to drink, he just rolls over and starts snoring as soon as he gets into bed.

He's well aware of his shortcomings though, and he's had prostate problems for a while. He wakes up in the morning standing to attention and that's why he wants me before getting up to go to the toilet, but I really don't think he gets any pleasure from it. You could even say he's in pain. I can tell from the expression on his face. It's an artificial hard on, after all, but he can't seem to give it up either. It's as if he gets frustrated with himself.

I've got really bored of all this strained sex, but I can't say no either. There's a bond between us based on our unhealthy and rather long past. Would I have been able to get to where I am now if I hadn't met him? Whenever I ask myself that, I always give him the benefit of the doubt. He's the man who opened the door for me to that other life I was longing for. He's been very good to me . . .

Three weeks after our meal in Akmerkez, he came to the shop one morning, poked his head round the door and called out with a smirk, "How are you, madam?" There were sales assistants and customers there. "Hello, Orhan Bey," I said in a serious voice. But he came in, put his hands on my shoulders and kissed me on the cheeks without caring who was watching. In the few minutes he spent in the shop, he showered me with more compliments than I'd ever heard in my whole life.

That lunchtime, he and the boss went out for a meal. He popped into the shop again after they'd eaten and whispered in my ear, "Please, don't leave me orphaned in Istanbul this evening. I'll pick you up in front of Kurtoğlu Patisserie in Zincirlikuyu after work." And he went.

That evening, as I settled myself into the front seat of his luxury car, which I later found out was the only one of its kind in the whole of Istanbul, he told me I looked so beautiful. A new door was opening in my life.

As we were going down Bebek Hill, he asked me where I wanted to have dinner.

"Wherever you'd like," I replied.

"Let's go to the fish restaurant next to my hotel, then," he said.

He was staying at the Bebek Hotel, which had a classy bar downstairs. When we pulled up in front of it, he suggested having something to drink in the bar first. "I'll just pop upstairs and get changed," he said.

Everyone in the bar knew him. When he walked in, the headwaiter immediately came over, shook our hands and showed us to one of the tables next to the sea. It wasn't like anywhere I'd been to with Ufuk or Burçin. It was more dignified, but also warmer and the customers were mainly middle-aged.

When the waiter who came over to take our order and I asked for a Coke, Orhan jokingly frowned and chided me: "Now, that's the wrong answer, Zarife Hanım." Then he ordered a whisky on the rocks for himself and a tequila for me. I'd never had tequila before. When he noticed me staring at the slices of lemon and the salt that came on a small plate with it, he showed me how to drink it.

He was a smooth talker and he kept on talking. Before I'd even got halfway through my first glass, I'd already learned everything about him: his wife and two children in Izmir, how they were doing at school, his factory and how much he paid the people working there. He always looked into my eyes as he spoke. He noticed me looking away once or twice and asked, "Why do you do that? Your eyes are so beautiful I can't get enough of looking into them."

He complimented me on how beautiful the color of my hair was, how soft my skin was and how dainty my fingers were. I'd never heard such beautiful words before. I believed him when he said he was really happy being there with me.

My head started to spin after the second glass. Orhan was holding my right hand in his over the table and stroking it. I suddenly thought of Ufuk and reached out my other hand too. Don't ask me why! I've no idea. The waiter kept bringing drinks. It was as if a dense mist had descended over the bar. Everything around me seemed out of focus. The conversations on the neighboring tables just sounded like noise to me.

Orhan got up. "I'm going upstairs; you can come too if you like," he said. I followed him without saying anything. When we were in his room, he pointed to the bed and said, "I've worn you out with everything I've been telling you; why don't you relax for a bit?"

I lay down and fell into an endless void as soon as I closed my eyes. I couldn't move. I wanted to move my hands, my arms, my legs, but

I couldn't. I wanted to open my mouth, speak, scream, but my voice wouldn't come out. As I tumbled in the void, I could see thousands of lights. Thousands of lights, like those stars I would see shining so brightly in the sky on cloudless summer nights. Then, colors I'd never seen before and melodies I'd never heard before mingled with those lights. It was as if dancing among them as I fell. I didn't want them ever to end. I was afraid to open my eyes in case those delectable sights and sounds should suddenly vanish. At one point, I felt Orhan's hands on my body. He was caressing my face, my neck, my arms, my breasts, my stomach. I didn't want to wake up from this dream. I shut my eyes tightly while he was unbuttoning my blouse. I could feel his hot breath and the moistness of his lips on my skin. Then he took off my bra and started caressing and kissing my breasts, and I left myself go. I let myself go, knowing it, wanting it, enjoying it. I don't know when I finally drifted off into sleep. The last thing I remember was the pain I felt in my loins at one point amid a pleasure that I was experiencing for the first time.

In the morning, I woke up to the sound of Orhan's voice. He was standing at the foot of the bed stark naked. "Why didn't you tell me, babe?" he asked.

At first, I didn't understand what he meant. Then when I looked down to where he was looking, I saw the now dark brown clotted traces of my virginity on my legs. He asked me again.

"I wanted it . . ." I said.

At that moment, I felt that something inside me was lost and gone, that my brain was emptied, and that I was cleansed of all the emotions that had been smothering me.

"So this is what they call freedom," I said.

He was unnerved by how calm I was. "What's wrong with you?" he asked.

I shrugged my shoulders. What sort of answer could I possibly give? Whatever I said, he wasn't going to understand me. Actually, I didn't know what was wrong with me at that moment either. The only thing I knew was that the dreams of the future that I'd had together with my family and Ufuk, and the white wedding dress that Şükran insisted on making for me had both turned into memories that were left behind now.

One tear for each of them fell from my eyes as I thought of them.

"Are you crying?" he asked and lay down next to me. He held me tight. It was as if he was overcome by a feeling of guilt, as if he was being crushed under the weight of it. His talking, his behavior, his caresses were different now. He was breathing in the smell of my hair, kissing me on my forehead and my cheeks, stroking my back and my hands as if he was stroking a newborn baby's skin. "You became my wife yesterday night," he said softly in my ear. "You're my real wife."

This had no effect on me, but I couldn't work out why not. I listened to him without saying anything, without showing any reaction, without affirming. That morning I learned that his wife was the daughter of a wealthy relative and he'd found out on his wedding night that she wasn't a virgin, but he couldn't say anything because her father had put up the capital for his factory in Izmir. They later had children, but his marriage was an unhappy one.

I sensed he was telling me all this so I'd forgive him, but I wasn't paying any attention. The balance between us had shifted in my favor the moment he realized he'd taken my virginity. The man who until yesterday I'd known as strong and supremely self-confident was resting his head on my arm and telling me jokes, trying to make me smile, like a naughty boy doing all sorts of cute things to hide something he'd done wrong from his mother. I felt sorry for him. I put my fingers in his hair and as I stroked his head, I said with a mother's tenderness, "Hush. Stop talking."

It was almost nine when I left the hotel and got in a taxi to go to Mecidiyeköy. I felt nauseous when I remembered that I hadn't eaten anything for twenty-four hours. I stopped the taxi and bought two *poğaças* from the snack bar at the corner of the road that goes up to Etiler. As I was eating them, I thought about what had happened that night. I didn't have the slightest pang of regret for what I'd done. I'd willingly given myself to Orhan. I'd done the best thing I could have done to free myself from the ambivalent feelings I'd been grappling with for weeks; now I'd no longer have to shuttle back and forth continually between the life I lived and the longings I felt for other lives. His behavior in the morning just went to prove it. When I was sitting at the edge of the bed putting my tights on, he knelt down in front of me and begged, "No, please, don't put them on."

I'd already got them halfway up and he pulled them off me, lay down on the floor and started kissing my feet and toes. At that moment, he seemed like an animal in its death throes. As he was sucking my big toe, he was rubbing himself off with one of his hands.

When I started to get up, he pleaded, "Don't go, stay a bit longer!"

I didn't listen. I put my right foot on his chest and said, "It's not like we're not going to see each other again."

I got dressed quickly and left.

We met for the next three nights in a row. We left the hotel together on the Saturday morning he was going back to Izmir. As we were parting, he said, "I'm going to miss you like crazy. You've caught me in your spell."

I gave him a peck on the cheek and without saying a word walked towards the taxi the hotel doorman had called.

13

When I got home, I found my mother and my youngest brother in front of the TV watching an old Kemal Sunal[2] film. She leaped up when saw me and gave me a hug, saying, "We really missed you."

She'd believed the story I'd told her over the phone on Tuesday evening about Customs and Excise raiding the company and me having to work late for the next four days and crashing at a friend's who lived near the shop.

"And I really missed all of you too, mum," I replied.

I got changed in my brothers' room and went and sat with them. They were having a normal Saturday just like the ones I'd known since my childhood. It must have been because it was the first time I'd been so far from home, but everything around me seemed older, more neglected, more worthless.

I felt sorry for my mum: she'd resigned herself to her fate without complaining and was living out her days in this poor slum, but I wasn't going to live like her. I'd rebelled against that cheap life they wanted to impose on me, as they had on her, and I'd taken my first steps on the path to another life. I'd chosen it deliberately and willingly and now there was no turning back. I was determined to walk down that road until the end.

I'd left this house as a timid, directionless girl who continually

---

2. Kemal Sunal: One of the most famous comic actors in Turkey.

wavered between her life of four days ago and the life she wanted to live; I'd returned as a determined, strong, self-confident woman. I'd met Orhan at just the right time. If someone else instead of Orhan had crossed my path that day, I might have given myself to him too. Because there was no way the moment could be held off. It was just chance that it happened to be Orhan who was accompanying me on my new path.

He'd fallen in love with me. On the second night, he held my arms and gazed into my eyes as we were watching the Bosporus together on the hotel balcony and said, "I love you more than you'll ever know."

He'd wander around me like a spoiled pet cat, touching me, rubbing against me suggestively and expecting me to respond to his love. Once again, I realized that my body was a weapon I could use against men. If I used it well, I could get Orhan to do anything I wanted, but I wasn't going to—not because I couldn't, but because the time hadn't come. I was like a hunter: I had my weapon aimed at my quarry and I was waiting for the best moment to shoot. I'd come further in four or five weeks than Burçin and the friends she often mentioned had in years. I'd made a wealthy, powerful man—the sort they looked for but hadn't been able to find, the sort they wanted to reach but couldn't—fall in love with me.

If that's being a whore, then it was always latent within me, Bülent Bey. You see, if I didn't have that spirit within me, how else could I have made that decision? How else could I have turned my back so easily on the values I'd held dear until that day? How else could I have just dropped the boyfriend, who I knew loved me and with whom I'd built dreams for a future together? How else could I have slept with a man who was married with children and who I'd seen a grand total of three times? I'm right, aren't I?

At one point, I felt like saying to my mother, "You know, mum, your daughter's a whore now. She broke herself in with a father of two children." What would the poor woman have done? How would she have reacted?

When the film was over and the adverts began, she went into the kitchen to wash up the breakfast things. I joined her a bit later. I put my hands on her hips and pressed my cheek against hers. "You're the best mum in the world," I said.

14

The next day was Sunday. I was going to meet Ufuk in Üsküdar and then we were going to the other side to have lunch with a married friend of his who lived in Fındıkzade. After that, we were all going to go up to Beyoğlu together and meet up with our other friends.

I woke up early. In the middle of the night after everyone had gone to bed, I'd lain up for hours thinking about how I'd tell him it was over between us. We hadn't even had the tiniest of rows since we met. He'd never uttered a single unkind word. He was good, honest and straight as a die. Can you just roll up in front of someone like that and say out of the blue, "Sorry, mate, you're dumped. You're on your own now!"

Would I be able to say that? The more I thought about it, the more depressed I got. My face and body felt feverish. Somehow, I had to find a way of telling him the truth without offending or hurting him.

"The truth?" I asked myself. What was the truth? Was it the truth to tell him I didn't love him any more? I still loved him.

So was it the truth to tell him I'd met another man and slept with him? Was that it, my truth? And what would happen to everything I'd lived until then? Weren't they my truths too? If I'd never encountered them and lived through them, would I have longed for other truths? Wanting to be different, wanting to change, that was a truth too. Maybe the most important, the most fundamental truth of all. Can there be any truth that's more important for us than deciding to be another person, than turning the life we live into another life? If this is the most fundamental and significant truth, then does it matter what steps I've taken and have left to take on my chosen path? At the end of the day, Burçin, Orhan and me sleeping with Orhan were each just steps to take me to another life, to a life I definitely want to live.

When Ufuk saw me, he asked, "What's wrong? You're as white as a sheet."

"I didn't sleep a wink last night," I said. Before he could ask why, I added, "I want to talk to you, but what I'm about to say isn't pleasant."

He could tell that something bad was coming from the way I didn't look away, the sour note in my voice and the way I was fidgeting nervously while speaking.

"Are we going to talk here?" he asked.

"Why don't we walk for a bit," I said.

We walked for a while along the shore towards Şemsipaşa Mosque without saying a word. He was dying to know what I was going to say. As we got closer to the mosque, he couldn't stand it any longer. "Is what you've got to say really so important?" he asked. "Important enough to keep Sevinç and Mustafa waiting at the table?"

I was only concentrating on what I was going to tell him, so I couldn't think about anything else.

"Yes," I said, "it really is very important."

"Come on then, just say whatever it is you've got to say!" he exploded. "You're driving me mad not telling me."

We stopped and stood next to the mosque wall that extended up to the sea.

"I'm not exactly sure how to put all of this into words," I started. "You'll be really shocked and upset at what you're about to hear, and believe me, I'm very upset too, but it's something we've got to go through."

I looked at him to gauge his reaction. He seemed to be concentrating.

"I've decided to change my life," I continued. "I want to build another life for myself. I don't know if I'll be able to do it, but I'm sure as hell going to try. I have to. If don't, if I'm not strong enough to try, life will have no meaning left for me. I'll be embittered to myself, the people around me, everyone. And once I've become embittered to life, I'll be of no use to anyone. How can I explain? I don't want to end up like my mother or like your mother; I don't want to live like them. It's got nothing to do with being a good or a bad person. Can you understand what I'm saying? My mother and your mother are both very good people, but I can't see any sparkle in their lives, but I like sparkle, lights and colors. I long for a life that can give me that . . ."

He interrupted me.

"And you're trying to say that I don't have a place in this life?" he asked.

"That's right," I said. "You don't, unfortunately. You're a very good person and I cherish you. You're my first love. It's not about you. We've had such a beautiful time together. You made me feel so happy, but as the longing inside me for another life grows, I'm going to hurt you and upset you. That's what I'm really scared of; I really don't want that to happen."

He looked like he'd seen a ghost. His cheeks bulged as he gritted his teeth. "Can't we try a bit longer?" he asked sadly.

"No," I said. "It would do us both more harm than good. You'll look for the Zarife you know and love in me, but I'm not that girl any longer."

He went on the offensive: "This must be Burçin's doing."

"No," I retorted. "She might have shown me a door I was looking for but couldn't find. After I'd decided to open that door, what difference does it make if it was Burçin who showed me it or someone else?"

I paused for a moment.

"Don't you ever watch TV or read newspapers and magazines?" I asked. "They're full of pictures of those bright, shiny, colorful lives you always turn your back on and want nothing to do with. You might not want to be in those pictures, but I do, I really do, and I'll do whatever it takes to be able to. I'm going to force myself to, so that in the future I won't regret not doing it. I'm going to do it by myself. And if my longings are strong enough to make me change my life and transform myself, then I have to take sole responsibility for it too. It's my life that's going to change, after all, and I'll bear the consequences."

He looked at me intently and asked, "Is there someone else?"

I'd been expecting that question from the beginning.

"No!" I replied without hesitating. "Does there always have to be someone else in a break up?"

We were silent. After a while, he said, "If that's all you've got to say, then you listen to me for a bit."

His chin was quivering. His eyes were damp.

"I realize what I'm about to say won't save our relationship," he said. "Because you've already made up your mind. But I want you to know the feelings that I had for you, that blossomed inside me and that I nourished. I don't think I have to tell you that listening to you wounded my heart and tore me up inside. It must have shown on my face. And I'm not going to tell you again how much I love you either. I just want to tell you that the path you've chosen is a very difficult one, and don't think I'm just saying that to make you change your mind. I know you very well: you're very fragile in fact. And maybe it really isn't important who lead you astray or who guided to you onto your new path, but I have to tell you that it's not the right path. I don't know if it's right or wrong for other people, but I do know that it's not right for you. Of course, you're right when you say you only live once. That applies to you and me both. But isn't being a couple when two people who love and desire each other bring their lives together and complete each other? I've loved you ever since I met you and I thought you loved me too. You've always been in all my dreams for the future. I'd got to the point where I couldn't imagine my tomorrow without you. We were going to share our lives, and you wanted that too, as much as I did. I wish you'd told me earlier that you'd changed your mind and longed for another life. Listening to you just now, I thought to myself, if you hadn't met me, if we hadn't loved each other enough to dream of building a future together, would you still have wanted to change like this? Would it even have crossed your mind? I think me being the first man in your life has got something to do with it as well. If instead of me it had been someone who was closer to that life you long for, I don't suppose you would have been so hard on yourself. Me appearing on the scene turned out to be a stroke of bad luck for you, really bad luck. But how could I possibly have known?"

My tears welled up as I was listening to him. I'd been expecting him to lose his temper or become aggressive or even to start hurling abuse at me, but what he'd said made me emotional. He was right. If he hadn't traced out a future for me with clear boundaries, if he hadn't made me aware of the limits of the life we'd live together, how could I have compared what I could have with what I longed for? As I was thinking about this, he started speaking again.

"It's easy for me because I never lied to you. I never promised you more than I'd be able to do. Maybe my family's slightly better off than yours, but apart from that, there's no real big difference between our lives. My parents both really liked you. I thought I could offer you a loving home environment. Hand in hand, shoulder to shoulder, we could have built ourselves a happy life, a modest and simple life, but a decent one. But I see you've wandered very far from that kind of life, the life that I want. Too far for me to reach, too far for me to want to reach. I hope everything turns out how you want it to. I hope one day you find the happiness you're looking for."

He gave me hug and kissed me on the cheeks and then said good-bye and walked off towards the main road.

I watched him until he disappeared. Then I sank to my knees and sobbed.

Ufuk was the most honorable man I'd ever met.

15

On a mild April day ten months later, Orhan and I touched down at Antalya Airport. I had no idea of the surprise that was in store for me . . .

I'd already been very surprised when he told me we were going to Antalya that weekend because he'd generally spend his weekends in Izmir with his family. When he saw the look on my face, he explained it away saying, "It's a bit of business and a bit of pleasure. We're going to the opening of a boutique on Friday and then we'll have the rest of the weekend to ourselves."

I made up an excuse and got two days off work. We spent Thursday night, as usual, in the Bebek Hotel and got a taxi to Yeşilköy Airport the next morning. I was very nervous because I'd never been on a plane before. I told Orhan and he stroked my cheek. "Don't be scared, babe," he said, "I'm here with you." He held my hand as we were taking off and didn't let it go of it again until we landed in Antalya . . .

We'd be together every time he came to Istanbul and he'd introduced me to his friends there. They were all successful and wealthy men like he was and they all had young, pretty girlfriends like he did. These girls generally came from poor families like I did. In time, I got to know a lot of them and even became friends with a few of them. We'd meet and talk about our jobs, clothes, the cinema or the lives of famous singers. When the conversation turned to men, everyone would start bitching about their lovers, but I'd keep my mouth shut.

Most of them lived in small luxury flats in good parts of Istanbul, rented and furnished by the men they were seeing, and they got a very generous amount of spending money. When they went out shopping with their lovers, they'd come back home with expensive gifts.

The men they were seeing had been worn out by their long marriages. The girls added color to their monotonous, hollow and faded lives. The girls' vigor, their *joie de vivre* and their energy would take the men back to their youth, quicken them and reconnect them to life.

The Istanbul party scene was full of young girls competing for the attentions of famous, wealthy men. There was nothing they wouldn't try to get one step ahead, be the center of attention, and appear in the papers or on TV with famous singers, footballers or rich businessmen. It was a market that had its own standards, rules and mechanisms where a girl who was seen with a famous man would immediately go up in value. The girls knew this, so they were ready to give everything they had to climb into one of the jeeps lined up in the car park of an expensive bar, restaurant or meyhane, or go to the parties held in luxury studio flats or on private boats touring the Bosporus. My girlfriends in my new life called them "little whores" (the men referred to them as chicks) and they'd put a lot of effort into keeping these little whores, and there were always more and more of them, away from their boyfriends. They'd have meals and parties for each other in their houses, but if they absolutely had to go out, they'd go to fish restaurants or meyhanes in Beyoğlu where those little whores didn't usually go.

Orhan wasn't too fussed about the party scene, so I never really had these kinds of problems. When he came to Istanbul, he'd want to spend most of his time with me. He had issues. He'd never been able to get over the fact that he'd launched his business career with his father-in-law's money, even though that was years ago now. He thought his wife was too used to getting her own way and he didn't like how she behaved, but he also knew that he couldn't change her.

When we first met, I had no idea how to react when he complained about his wife, so I just kept quiet and listened to what he was telling me. But one time after he'd poured his heart out at length again, he asked me, "Aren't you going to say anything?"

At that moment, for some reason, I felt I had to defend her. "You shouldn't be so hard on the mother of your two children!" I said. This had a great effect on him. He took my hands: "Zarife by name, Zarife by nature,"[3] he said. From that day on, whenever he'd complain about his wife, I'd always find some way of defending her.

Men like Orhan are in the situation where the feelings they have for their wives have degenerated over time into hatred, but for various reasons they can't break out of their marriages and they know they never will be able to. You might not realize that they expect their girlfriends to be understanding and respectful about it. This means you've got to approve their past and accept things as they really are. Defending his wife shows you're understanding about the marriage he's trapped in. And in this kind of relationship, that's an important piece of evidence to show that you accept him as he is.

The respect and understanding I had for his wife and his marriage raised me even higher in his estimation. I'd become an angel in his eyes. "You're my angel. I've finally found you and I'm afraid of losing you," he would say to me.

I'd heard from my friends that every man has a weak point, but it's extremely difficult and can sometimes take a very long time to find. Finding Orhan's so quickly really was a huge stroke of luck for me.

---

3. Zarife: Elegant, tasteful, refined in Turkish.

And I understood just what it meant from the expensive presents I began to get often.

Every time he came to Istanbul, it was my role to listen while he told me about the latest dramas and tragedies he'd had with his wife. As he was pouring out his woes to me, I'd interrupt at a convenient point so the next time we met he'd come bringing a pearl necklace, a gold chain or a diamond ring for me. All I had to do was say something like, "But you're so cruel to Müjgan Hanım, darling," or "More than anything else, you've got to respect the fact that she's a mother."

I'd learned from friends who had experience in this kind of relationship that I should speak about his wife respectfully and always add the word "Hanım" as a mark of respect after her name. The girls would use the most scathing and insulting words you've ever heard to describe their lovers' wives when they were chatting amongst themselves, but would speak about them in respectful tones in front of the men . . .

At Antalya Airport, a chubby middle-aged man with glasses who Orhan introduced as his accountant, Erdinç Bey, met us. He drove us straight to Cumhuriyet Street, where the shop was, without stopping off at the hotel. The shop had a sign saying "Elegance Leather Shop". Cumhuriyet Street itself was a busy street with quite a few other shops selling carpets, watches, souvenirs and designer clothes as well as three small restaurants. The street that opened onto it was pretty close to the marina.

The front of the shop was decked out with dark green decorative plants in the wreathes, baskets of flowers and large flower pots that various people, organizations, banks and travel agents had sent.[4] The guests were talking to each other, nursing glasses in their hands. When Erdinç Bey went inside and announced we'd arrived, a young girl and

---

4. In Turkey, when a new business opens, it is customary for other businesses and local dignitaries to send floral displays.

a young man who I guessed must work in the shop because they were wearing T-shirts with "Elegance Leather" written on them came out to welcome us and asked if there was anything we wanted. I sensed something was going on from the almost fawning respect and attention they and the guests showed me.

After a short while, Orhan stood by the door and addressed the guests, who by now were spilling out from the pavement and onto the street. "Ladies and gentlemen, esteemed guests, dear friends, could I have your attention please for one minute?"

Once he'd got them listening, he called me over.

"I'd like to introduce you to the manager of our new Antalya branch and my partner, Zarife Hanım," he said. "She runs a shop belonging to a big wholesaler I work with in Istanbul, but she's Antalyan now."

I couldn't believe my ears. When the guests began to clap, I was so nervous my legs started trembling. I didn't know what I should say or do. Once I'd composed myself a bit, I stammered, "I really wasn't expecting this . . . It's such a big surprise . . . I don't know what to say . . . I'd like to thank Orhan Bey and all of you."

The guests congratulated me and wished me all the best. When everyone had gone, Orhan showed me round the storeroom and then took me to my modern office at the back of the shop. He called Didem and Mustafa in and told them they had to do what I told them. He gave various pieces of work-related advice.

If he'd asked me what I thought before he actually did all this, would I have said yes? Would I have been strong enough to say yes? I don't think so. The thought of taking on all those responsibilities and living alone far from my family in an unfamiliar city where I didn't know anyone would have frightened me and I'd definitely have said no. He didn't say anything because he knew that's how I would react. He brought me here and left me in front of a closed door that I couldn't refuse to open. Now I had no other choice but to open it and go in.

Contrary to what I'd been expecting, my family immediately warmed to the idea of me working in Antalya. They were all very happy when they found out that I was going to be managing a shop on three times my old salary and living in a company flat and that my contribution to the family budget would go up. It didn't occur to any of them to ask how I'd found the job and I didn't tell them about Orhan or about me getting a share of the profits on top of my basic salary either. My boss, though, was quite alarmed at first because there'd be no one to look after the shop until he found a suitable replacement, but when he realized in the course of the conversation that Orhan was behind everything, he didn't try to stop me. Still, when I went to collect my final pay packet on the last day, he just said, "Be careful, my girl. You never know where you stand with Orhan Bey. But anyway, all the best."

On the last Sunday in April, I landed at Antalya Airport carrying a big suitcase. Erdinç Bey met me again and took me to the flat where I'd be living. It was at the start of the coastal road that went to Kemer.

"Unwind today and we'll meet in the shop tomorrow morning," he said, stuffed quite a thick envelope into my hand and went.

The last time Orhan was in Istanbul, he'd said, "The flat will be our love nest. I hope you like it." It was on the top floor of a new three-story building that looked out onto the sea. It was a nice two-bedroom flat with light, pastel furniture. On our way from the airport, Erdinç Bey said that Orhan Bey had chosen all the furniture and the bathroom and kitchen fittings himself. "He thinks very highly of you, hanımefendi."

I could tell from his tone of voice, the way he looked at me and all the respect he showed me that he knew about me and Orhan, but I pretended I hadn't noticed. After he'd gone, I went round the bed-rooms, the living-room, the kitchen and the bathroom. I opened the cupboards and looked inside them; I examined everything that was in the house.

The envelope he'd given me contained a small piece of paper with the word "advance" written on it and quite a large sum of money. I unpacked and after I'd hung all my clothes up in the bedroom, I got undressed. As I lay naked on the large, comfortable double bed, I said out loud, "God really loves me, but I really love myself too."

I'd come quite far in my new life in a short space of time. My old friends from school and home appeared before my eyes. I had a much more beautiful and colorful world than they did. When I cast my eyes on my necklaces, rings and earrings, which I'd carefully arranged on the mirrored dressing table, I purred, "And they're just the beginning . . ."

My new job, the house Orhan called our love nest, the presents I received, the money that was so exciting to count . . . They were the beginning. The beginning of a bigger life that I'd have one day in the future. I thought to myself: if I hadn't made that decision in the hotel that night, could I have been where I am now? Everything came at a price, of course. I had paid with my body and I was still paying for the things I'd get in the future. I had no regrets about what I'd done. As I was thinking about all this, my right hand went down between my legs by itself and I started caressing the lips of what Orhan called "my little box" when he was kissing it.

It was as if my body became even more beautiful with each day that passed.

Erdinç Bey picked me up early the next morning and took me to the shop. Didem and Mustafa met me at the door. Erdinç Bey and I had tea and poğaças in my office. He was very measured in his behavior. He gave me detailed information about work. He said that selling to the public wasn't an issue for a while because there was still two months to go until the tourist season, so it would be more appropriate for me to concentrate on wholesale customers for the time being. He was a very meticulous man. He had compiled a list of all the customers in Antalya and the surrounding area who had bought from Orhan in the last two years. As he handed it to me, he said I'd be getting five percent on wholesale sales. "You'll make good money in Antalya, hanımefendi. It'll be worth your while having come here," he said.

I was about to ask how I would get to the customers outside Antalya, but he seemed to have read my mind and said, "Orhan Bey has put a car at your disposal too. Mustafa will drive you until you get your license."

As we spoke, I could tell he was a close associate of Orhan and had worked with him for years, even if he didn't really want to show it.

I spent the next few days visiting customers. They were mainly small and middle-sized leather shops and gift shops, or else boutiques in holiday resorts that were only open for the high season and catered mainly to foreign tourists. Although I had no previous marketing experience, I got over my initial nervousness after the first couple of visits. I acted relaxed as if I'd been doing the job for a long time. The owners of the businesses I went to were mainly men and that played its part too. They liked having an attractive young woman in front of them. Of course, when they found out I was from Istanbul, they started behaving completely differently. They placed orders for goods they might never have thought of buying under normal circumstances.

They were depressed and felt hemmed in by their everyday lives. They had dreams of escaping from it all but they knew they'd never be able to make them come true. They were sick of bumbling along in the home-work-meyhane triangle for months on end in a city that became lifeless and faded when the tourists left. They were sluggish as if they'd just come out of hibernation with the coming of spring, but they came to life when they saw me sitting across from them and recalled that they did have something gathering cobwebs between their legs after all. They agreed with every word that came out of my mouth and did whatever they could to make me like them. Every time I laughed or smiled, they thought they were in with a chance. I hadn't thought I'd be able to get to grips with marketing so easily. I'd always get asked out to dinner or for a couple of drinks by half the customers I visited. But I turned them all down, without offending or hurting them, and always leaving the gates of hope ajar.

Erdinç Bey would pop into the shop in the morning and take the previous day's orders. He was surprised at how good my sales were. Before two weeks were over, he said, "It seems Orhan Bey was right, hanımefendi. You really are fantastic."

Orhan was very pleased with my work too. He'd call me on my mobile each day to congratulate me. Once when he called, I told him I really missed him, but I soon wished I hadn't after he told me how busy they were in the factory getting ready for the summer season. That was the first time I noticed that he wasn't acting like my lover, but like my boss in the short phone calls we'd been having since I came to Antalya. I didn't want to read anything into it, but I had a sense of foreboding.

As the days passed, I felt more and more lonely. I'd go to the shop each morning, give Erdinç Bey the orders from the day before and go out on customer visits with Mustafa. In the evening, I'd come home worn out and have a bite to eat before sitting down in front of the TV until my eyes closed. I hadn't seen Orhan for almost a month. I thought of going to Istanbul for two or three days at some point to see my family and friends again, but I put it off until some time in the future because leaving Antalya even for a few days would disrupt my work.

I was intrigued one morning when Erdinç Bey said he'd be going to visit Kuşadası, Marmaris and Bodrum the next day, so I'd have to prepare and send the lists of orders for Izmir myself.

"What do you mean, visiting them?"

"Ah, didn't you know?" he said. "Orhan Bey has branches there as well, and they're all run by successful, hardworking hanımefendis like you, but you're much more successful than any of them."

The moment I heard this, I understood why since the first day we met, he'd had a mysterious expression on his face every time he called me hanımefendi. I wasn't, as I wanted to make myself believe, Orhan's one and only, his little wife who tragically had appeared so late in his life. I was just one of his mistresses. I'd never used that word before. I felt insulted and betrayed, angry and outraged all at the same time. I gritted my teeth so Erdinç Bey wouldn't notice and so I wouldn't scream.

When he'd gone, I told Didem to cancel that day's appointments and I rushed outside, leapt into a taxi and went home. I got into bed and cried my heart out. When I was feeling a bit better, I plucked up the courage to call Orhan and asked him why he'd lied to me.

"I didn't want to upset you," he said. "Besides, what's there to get all angry about?"

I was left speechless by how matter-of-fact he was about it.

I couldn't settle for being just any woman in Orhan's life. But there was nothing I could do either, apart from appearing to accept things. I couldn't drop everything and run back to my old little world once more, not while I was still at the beginning of the path that would take me to that other life I'd spent years dreaming of. According to

Erdinç Bey's calculations, the advance together with my bonus from the orders I'd got in the three weeks I'd been here was more than I earned in three months in Istanbul. With my one-third share in the profits from retail sales, which would start when the tourist season did, my earnings would go up two or three times. I thought about it for two days and decided to stay in Antalya and throw myself into my work again.

I never brought up the subject with Orhan again. As before, I would thank him and hang up after listening to him praise my work each day. But then in one conversation he said to me, "There's something different about you: it's as if you don't miss me at all." I couldn't control myself.

"You were the one who made me forget how to miss you!" I shrieked.

We had a small row. He said he was still very busy and couldn't leave Izmir, so I said, "Please, don't lie to me. I know you were in Kuşadası two days ago and I know everything you did there."

I'd heard he was there from Erdinç Bey, who was back from his trip round the Aegean. The shop manager there was a young, recently separated woman from Izmir called Çiğdem. While Erdinç Bey was in Kuşadası, Orhan had come too, picked up Çiğdem and then the three of them had gone out to dinner to talk over day-to-day business. Erdinç Bey had set off for Marmaris towards midnight. I knew full well that Orhan wouldn't have dropped Çiğdem off at home and spent the night alone in a hotel. He tried to defend himself, but I interrupted him.

"Don't cover up your lies with even more lies," I yelled. "That's the last thing you need! And if you think I'm jealous of that bitch, you're wrong. If I was going to be jealous, I'd have been jealous of your wife first."

That same week, I bumped into Orhan as I was walking out of the shop on Friday evening. He gave me a hug and kissed me on the cheeks. There was a tall, elegant, attractive, black haired woman with him. I froze.

"I thought I'd surprise you," he said and introduced her: "This is Çiğdem Hanım, manager of our Kuşadası branch."

At first, I didn't know how to react. I thought I could feel the color drain from my face. Which woman could have accepted a situation like that? I felt like jumping on the bastard and tearing his face to shreds, but I regained my composure, reached my hand out to Çiğdem and said in a cold voice, "Pleased to meet you. Welcome to Antalya."

We went into the shop and hung around inside. After a while I said, "I guess you're hungry. Wouldn't you like to have something to eat by the sea?" If I hadn't asked, Orhan would have . . .

We walked towards the marina in complete silence and went into one of the newly opened fish restaurants. Orhan sat down next to Çiğdem and started to tell how they had scared a shepherd on the way here when they drove into his flock of sheep. I was really pissed off at how he could be so calm, as if nothing had happened, and how he could laugh. Çiğdem, though, was more on edge and subdued. She kept looking towards the sea at the boats in the marina so she wouldn't have to make eye contact with me. Orhan could feel the tension at the table, so he was leaping from subject to subject trying to lighten the atmosphere.

The first sip of my rakı burned my throat. I really don't like drinking, but I'd made up my mind: I was going to have as much as I could that evening to drink through my anger. As I was picking out the bones from the fish on my plate, my glance fell on Çiğdem's hands. She had smooth skin and long, slender fingers. Her nail varnish was a dark brownish burgundy. As I was looking at her nails, I thought about the first day I met Orhan in Homestore in Akmerkez. It was almost a year ago. So many things in my life had changed since then and most of that was due to the man sitting opposite me who was being fed fish by his girlfriend. He had opened the gates to paths going to different, beautiful lives. On the other side of those gates, I'd met quite a few girls like me who also longed for different, beautiful lives and I'd learned a lot from them. As I lived and learned, my walk, my laugh, my behavior, my clothes, my makeup, everything had changed. Orhan had turned me into the woman I'd always wanted to be. I could forgive him. There were still more things I wanted to get to know, experience, attain and obtain. I didn't want to stop and go back. I was afraid of being the old Zarife again. And it wasn't as if Orhan was my goal in life, the last stop I wanted to get to on my path. I was going to bury my jealousy and anger inside me and forgive him. I had to.

My head was spinning from all the rakıs I'd drunk. Çiğdem was pretty plastered too. The more she drank, the more her unease disappeared and the more uninhibited she became. She called me sweetheart and darling when she spoke. And Orhan was like a dog with two tails. Every time our glasses became empty, he'd have them refilled saying, "Drink up, my beauties!"

At one point, he held Çiğdem's hand in his on the table and started stroking it. She leaned her head on his shoulder. I remembered the first time we went to the bar of the Bebek Hotel. He held my hand in his and stroked it too that evening.

The year's gone so quickly, I thought to myself. "Here's to our friendship always being so beautiful."

They joined in my toast and raised their glasses. We downed our rakıs. A short while later, Orhan said, "We'll continue at home now," and we left.

We got a big bottle of rakı from the restaurant and took a taxi to my place. Çiğdem really liked the house. "I hope you enjoy living here, darling. It's so nice. I hope I'll have a house like this too one day," she said. Then she went and sat down on the sofa next to Orhan. When I came back from getting the rakı glasses from the kitchen, I found them smooching. "Come and sit with us too!" Orhan said and, like a well-trained dog, I did.

He immediately put his arm round me, pulled me towards him and kissed me on the lips. Then he started to caress our legs and our breasts. At one point, my eyes met Çiğdem's. There was alarm, fear and shame in them. It was obvious she'd never had a night like this before either. All we could do was take refuge in alcohol. We let ourselves go. We surrendered to our hopes like the hundreds of innocent-looking women I'd seen in late-night films who regretted what they'd done when they'd sobered up.

At first, I didn't know what to do. I felt a mixture of fear and shame. My sexual experience was limited to shagging Ufuk and Orhan. Alcohol is your greatest friend in situations like this. It stops your brain and frees your body. I let myself go too. I didn't think anything as the three of us went through to the bedroom together, as we got undressed, as we had sex.

16

You really don't know what being a whore means, Bülent Bey. That's why I'm telling you everything about my life so candidly. I'm not hiding anything from you. If you can understand me, then you'll be able to understand what being a whore means too. Because you think it's a momentary action, an appearance reflecting that action, but it's not; being a whore, whether you're a woman or a man, is a choice, a way of life you freely choose.

No one set any traps in front of me to turn me into a whore. No one pushed me onto the slippery slope; no one dragged me into the quagmire or caught me in their web. Life's not a film! Orhan didn't force me to do anything either. He even got really nervous when he saw the streaks of dried blood between my legs the morning after our first night together. He asked me why I hadn't told him. I didn't doubt his sincerity for one moment.

And it was me who wanted to break up with Ufuk and be with Orhan. I left Ufuk so I could escape from a narrow, boring, colorless future. He was an obstacle in my path and I embraced Orhan to get over that obstacle. I embraced him so I could burn my bridges and close the doors behind me and not go back, not be able to go back, ever again. He's got absolutely nothing to answer for in any of this. He's really just a big child looking for toys and finding new ones when they get old, and he wants lots of toys . . . He's built a life where he can have as many as he wants whenever he wants. He's only got a mind for his business and for between his legs. He doesn't know what the theatre is. He doesn't go to the cinema or to concerts. He doesn't read books, and if you're wondering about the newspapers, he just glances at them, that's all. And that suited me down to the ground. I became one of his favorite toys. One of the toys he could play with when he felt like it and could find every time he looked.

I first realized I was his toy a year after we met, the day he brought Çiğdem to Antalya. The moment I saw her with him, I could have left everything and gone back to Istanbul if I'd wanted to, but I didn't. My expectations from life turned out to be stronger than my pride!

Like I said, alcohol helps you a lot in situations like that when you're pretending not to care, leaving everything to chance and ridding yourself of burdens, but I never used alcohol as an excuse. If I did, I'd have told you I regretted what I'd done and was ashamed of myself when I woke up the next morning, but I didn't say that. Because I didn't feel any regret or shame. Quite the opposite in fact, I felt much more alive, more vigorous and more robust than before.

That morning, Çiğdem and I went to the bathroom hand in hand, laughing and joking. Orhan was trying to rinse off his tiredness under the shower and we shoved him into the bathtub and joined him. We were both ready to give him whatever he wanted, and more besides, not to end up as one of those toys that gets old and thrown to one side. To stay in the game, you have to follow the rules, whatever they are, or else you're doomed from the start. I learned the rules well in my early years. I play the game masterfully, but Çiğdem didn't know how to play. She couldn't become a whore, I mean. She went back to Izmir a few months later and married a hairdresser. Now she lives in Bayraklı and has two children. It really isn't easy to deal with the little whores who'd give anything to join in the game and do the most unimaginable things to do so. Çiğdem couldn't deal with them.

I know so many girls who turn themselves into toys to try and break down the doors that lead to other beautiful lives. The keys to those doors are in the hands of men and girls trample over each other to be able to get to them. You're a journalist: you'll know better than I do. Parents take their daughters by the hand and put them in beauty contests, they beg the judges, they shed tears just so their daughters can be models and become famous and earn a lot of money and find a rich man. You can see girls like that all over the newspapers and gossip programs. They do whatever it takes to catch people's eye, to be in the limelight and to be able to find a good buyer.

I learned in time that I had to be better than these little whores if I wanted to be able to see them off. I paid the price for being better, for being irresistible, so I wouldn't have to pull out or fall out of the game. I'm still paying it. That's why I satisfied Orhan's most outlandish requests without complaint. It really wasn't easy to be an object of his perversions and insatiability. Eventually though, I started to notice that sex was a form of relief, a form of oblivion, and I started to want those things I used to find deviant too.

If I've got anywhere today—and I've got a flat in Yeniköy with a sea view that I haven't let Orhan set foot in, a jeep parked outside, a not inconsiderable sum of money in the bank—I owe it all to my determination.

I expanded the leather business in Antalya much quicker than I'd been hoping. My view of men radically changed after Orhan brought Çiğdem over. First, I slept with the general manager of a big holiday resort. He rented me an empty shop at the entrance to the resort for a pittance. And other hotel managers, travel agents and tourist guides followed. Using my youth, enthusiasm and femininity, I opened branches in Belek, Kemer and Konyaaltı in only my second year. As the volume of my orders grew, I managed to bring the price of the stock I got from Orhan down by a lot too. I was now getting forty per cent of the profits from the total sales of five shops, together with the main shop in Antalya. By the end of the fourth year, I had enough money to buy a flat in Istanbul. One year later, I dissolved my business partnership with Orhan and set up my own company.

Now I own three big shops on the coastal strip between Antalya and Adana and six boutiques in holiday resorts that are only open during the high season. I'm well respected enough in the circles I move in now not to have to put myself about for business contacts. In the life I live, the more money you have, the more respect you get . . .

The TV images you mentioned in your article were filmed in a club in Etiler. We moved on there after dinner in the Balıkçı restaurant in Bebek. Orhan gave me one of those tiny pills in the car, saying, "Here, swallow!"

Once I'd had two gin and tonics on top of the rakıs I'd already had with the meal, I really let myself go. And those pills, they make you crazy. When I arrived, I had my hair in a bun, but I let it down and leapt onto the table with the music. At that moment, I felt like I was little Zarife dancing on the tables years ago at my aunt's wedding in Gelincik Reception Hall in Beykoz. I wanted the music to go on forever. I wanted everyone to clap and say, "What a pretty girl you are. You dance so beautifully."

When I sat back down, Orhan said, "All eyes were on you."

I felt dizzy. I leaned my head on his shoulder and cried for a while without knowing why.

He said, "Let's go and have fun somewhere else," and we left.

I didn't have the strength to walk. Two girls I didn't know took me by the arms. We left the club with Orhan in front and the three of us behind. One of them smiled and said, "Orhan Bey invited us to the party too!" But I was so far gone at that moment that I couldn't even ask what party she was talking about.

I took refuge in faded images of my mother and father, of Salih and Şükran and Ufuk. I was dancing among them and my black ringlets had fallen over my face. When I opened my eyes, I was in the Çırağan Hotel. The party was being held in one of the rooms with a sea view. We sat on the chairs by the window and on the wide bed for a while, waiting for housekeeping to bring what Orhan had ordered.

They were talented girls, the little whores that Orhan had invited along to unburden me. When there was a knock at the door, they immediately ran to wheel the trolley in. It had a plate of fruit, drinks and glasses on it. Orhan sat down on one of the chairs in front of the window, his whisky on the rocks in his hand, and the girls lay me down in the middle of the bed and undressed me, kissing and caressing me all the while.

When I woke up the next morning, Orhan and the girls had gone. As I thought about it, I felt sorry for those girls. It's not easy to have sex with a woman you don't know in front of a man who's watching you and playing with himself at the same time. I know because I've been in similar situations; I had no choice. It hurts when you feel you're being used. You try to hide and suppress how degraded you're feeling with artificial mirth and smiles that sit crookedly on your face. You have hopes and expectations you don't want to give up on, you can't let go of them, you can't get up and leave. And who knows what those girls expected from life.

So you see, you don't become a whore just by hitchhiking or by climbing onto tables and dancing. There are hundreds and thousands of girls in Istanbul who hitchhike and who climb onto tables and dance. Are they all whores? And where do you draw the line? Where do you start being a whore? Who draws the line?

Take a quick look at the tables around you. Can you tell me which of the women are whores and which ones aren't? What about the men? Which of these couples are getting ready to cheat on their spouses at this very moment? Which of them are plotting that? And out of them, which ones are doing it in return for something?

We've been sitting here together for three hours and our eyes have met so many times, but I haven't noticed the slightest note of disdain or contempt. I've told you all these things, but still, you somehow can't accept that I'm a whore. You wince every time I utter that word and you blush. You don't want people to say bad things about me because I don't match the image of a whore you've got in your head at all. You don't see that startled hitchhiker who got into your car seven years ago or that smashed young woman you saw on TV sitting opposite you. You're disappointed. Maybe now you even regret what you wrote, but there's absolutely no need to. You just need to know that being a whore is one of the ways people force life's hand and stretch the realities of life by risking everything for the sake of impossible hopes.

You snap at the point when the chasm between your hopes and your realities has got too deep, when you're tired and weary, when you feel you haven't got the strength to take another step, when you're overcome by the fear that life is about to slip out of your hands. You either submit or rebel.

I didn't have the strength to rebel. I snapped; I submitted. Or maybe I rebelled in the wrong direction. But now it's too late for me to think or wonder about that.

17

Orhan doesn't know I'm meeting you. He wouldn't want me to open up to a stranger and if he knew I was going to let you into his inner world, he'd have done all he could to try and stop me from coming here.

I lied to him. I told him I was going to see an old friend. As I was going out the door, he asked if we were going to see each other this evening.

"I don't know, I'll call you later," I said.

But I won't call him. Apart from work, we don't have very much left to talk about. It's been years since we've asked each other about our private lives or told each other anything that would strike a raw nerve. In this life, friendships, like love, start to wear thin very quickly. If it wasn't for our business relationship, I might never see him. But he doesn't want to lose me. Because he knows that if he does, he'd be losing a good customer too. And things aren't so different for me either. I have to look out for number one too. Maybe it would be easy to find new arms I could become a whore in, a new shoulder I could rest my head on and cry. But it's not so easy to find a new factory that would put up with all my whims or that I could get to postpone my checks and IOUs for two or three months with a single phone call. So as you see, our relationship is based on mutual self-interest.

Six months ago, I hired Erdinç Bey. He and Orhan had a disagreement about uninvoiced sales and he left. Anyone else would have objected to me snapping up their accountant, but all Orhan said was, "He's a good man, a hardworking man."

Erdinç Bey is very hardworking. He knows every inch of the Mediterranean region. For the past six months, he's been scurrying about between Antalya and Adana for me. He's taken a big weight off my shoulders. So now, I can come to Istanbul more often. I can withdraw to my house in Yeniköy and get away from it all.

Once or twice, Orhan has said that he'd like to come and see the house, but I wasn't having it. For a long time now, I've been able to stand on my own two feet living that other life I always longed for when I was younger, but it's so hollow! Would you believe that behind all those lights, that glitter, those colors that I dreamed about for years, there's nothing. No soul, no feeling, no love . . . I keep my door closed to Orhan and people like him so that absence of soul, feeling and love won't come into my house.

I bumped into Burçin in Nişantaşı the other day and we stood talking to each other for a bit. Ufuk got married two years ago apparently and he's got a kid. He's happy. Şükran's still single though. The poor thing's given up hope. I called her yesterday and she's coming to stay with me for a couple of nights this weekend. We'll kick off our shoes and have a good old natter.

At one time, I'd escape from the house so as not to hear the neighborhood gossip, but I've even started missing that too now. At least there's feeling, at least there's a soul in all that small talk and gossip I used to look down on. Our neighbors would tell each other about their loves, their hopes, their angers and their sorrows. Their joys and their pains were genuine. I sometimes really miss that life which I used to find so dull and monochrome that I wanted to run away from it.

I've reached the point now where I can tell myself to stop and not look down on what I see in my past and where I can even find it pleasant and good. There comes a time when it becomes easier to rid yourself of envy and jealousy. I haven't been jealous of anyone for some time now. I don't envy anyone. I don't want to compete with anyone.

It's been years since I've talked to anyone for so long and bared my soul. It's the first time I'm confronting myself so openly and deeply. I'm even thinking of drawing a line under my life at the point where I am now and making a fresh start, but that's so difficult. I know that from business. Before you can make a fresh start, you have to draw up a balance sheet first. You have to go through all your invoices, your income, your expenditure, your stock, your bank accounts, your debits, your credits item by item and put them in the books. You can't say you'll just put what you feel like in the books and ignore everything else! Or else you'll end up being a fraud.

Just as I want my company's balance sheet to be honest, I want my life's balance sheet to be honest too. Unfortunately, people can't cope with things when they're all correct and open. They want everyone to have the same kind of life and past as they do. If they find the slightest blemish on you, they pick you apart. But I don't have any unblotted pages in my copybook. I can't stand up to them and say come and take a look. I have to hide myself. That's how I protect myself. I don't have the strength to face people endlessly asking me why I did what I did.

I grew up surrounded by lies, Bülent Bey. Lots of my friends had started going out with boys while they were still at high school. In the environment we were brought up in, although families did want their daughters to get married and start a family as soon as they could, if their daughters were friends with boys, they'd get angry and beat them. In the eyes of fathers and brothers especially, the honor of the girl of the house was the family honor. They always kept an eye on their daughters and sisters, but the girls would always manage to find a way to be with boys. You could lie to your family by saying you were at a girlfriend's or visiting someone who was sick or going to study at school. Whenever something was forbidden, it would bring forth a new lie and each new lie would breed other lies.

The biggest fear girls had was ending up having to marry someone their families had found for them and not being able to say no because of the respect they had for their parents, so to avoid this they'd start searching themselves from a very early age.

I also had friends who were going out with several boys at the same time. They worked on the logic that if one didn't work out, another would, and saw it as a kind of insurance policy. In this case of course, they told similar lies to their boyfriends too because they didn't know yet which of them was the one. When they did marry one of them, they knew they'd have to make him feel like he was the first man in their life. Virginity by itself is no proof of a clean past, so starting from their wedding night, they'd begin to play the role of the innocent girl who learns everything for the first time from her husband, even though they'd had dozens of orgasms by various methods with several different boys. Most marriages built on these kinds of lies don't work out. They just don't.

When I was young though, I never lied, apart from one or two white lies. I deliberately avoided situations where I'd have to lie. Before and after Orhan, I always lived without lies too. I want to live without lies from now on as well.

Today I'm a successful businesswoman. I've learned a lot from life and I've read a lot of books recently. In my new circle in Istanbul, if I reached out my hand, there'd be quite a few men who'd want to hold it, men who respect me and who I could like too, but they only know me through my appearance and the respect they have for me is limited to that. What will happen later, when they hold my hand and ask me to tell them everything? Am I to explain away the last seven years of my life as a series of unexpected surprises and happy coincidences? What will happen to Orhan? What will happen to me putting up with him, obeying him and waiting on him hand and foot? How can I explain my business success and my shops without talking about him and those hotel managers, travel agents and yacht owners? Everything I've lived is my truth, isn't it, Bülent Bey? Can you extract yourself from your truths and pretend you've not lived through what you've lived? Just thinking about it scares me.

I'm not one of those women who sacrifice their own personalities so they can believe in the reality of the fake lives they've lived. That's why I can never lie. I don't lie. I don't want to lie, and I haven't lied to you. You haven't asked me a single question all these hours. You just listening to me has been helpful: you got me talking.

While confronting myself, I've noticed there are quite a few things in my life that I shouldn't tell everyone, that I shouldn't share with anyone, that I should hide and keep quiet about, things that only you know. I still have a long life ahead of me. I want to carry the hope of a fresh start inside me, but I've realized that I've got to solve the Orhan problem first. I don't know how I'll do it, but I can see that I won't be able to create a new life for myself without getting rid of him first. The door that opened with him will close with him as well. I paid the price when I opened that door and I'll pay the price too when I close it, if necessary. Maybe a much higher price . . .

The day might come when I'll need you to vouch for me. You won't turn me down, will you?

You won't.

You can take me out to dinner now if you like.

If you like.

Nişantaşı, April 2003